KAT DRUMMOND BOOK TWO

BLOOD CARTEL

NICHOLAS WOODE-SMITH

Copyright © 2019

Kat Drummond

ISBN: 9781694084200

Contents

Chapter 1.   Justice

Don't be a hero.

People won't like you for being one. You probably won't even like yourself for it. And it is the way of the world that all good deeds do not go unpunished.

But that is just how I see it. And I'm a bit biased. Anyone would be if they were the one standing in an old pre-Cataclysm era, grey courtroom, facing a stern-faced magistrate with a gavel the size of a troll's fist.

Slaying monsters is what I do but, apparently, metaphorical monsters are a bit more complicated. Sure, kill a few thousand zombies, ghouls and assorted undead and you get a medal and a (passable) paycheque, but put one necromancer in the ground and prepare to do time. Didn't matter if that necromancer had murdered hundreds of people. Didn't matter that he had risen most of them and made the animated corpses kill even more people. Didn't matter that he deserved to die.

There was the law, and then there was what is right. In my mind, I was on the right side. The law was on the other.

"Your name is Kat Drummond?" the magistrate asked.

"Yes," I replied. My lawyer, some pro-bono junior lawyer just off his last exam, was rocking side to side like he was playing hot potato with the soles of his feet. I'd spoken to him briefly and gotten only stutters. Didn't inspire confidence, but as was often the case with me, the more anxious he looked, the less anxious I felt. Happened a lot. If someone else was shaking in their boots, I was still as a statue. Maybe I was channelling my angst into them? Or maybe I knew that if they were scared, I needed to be brave. And right now, with the weight of the law pressing down on me, I needed to be very brave.

"Nineteen years old. Student at the University of Cape Town. Lives alone. No dependents," the magistrate continued to read off a dossier.

It wasn't like the court room dramas. No jury, first of all. Hope City didn't use juries. No cameras. No big fuss. Just a single security guard (who I could easily take down if I had a mind to), a magistrate, a public prosecutor and my lawyer. There was no audience. My friends, Trudie, Pranish and Andy, were all busy writing the same exam. Hopefully this sham of a case would be settled by the time my exams came up. Could always write a sup, but that required paperwork. I hate paperwork.

"On the 21st of April, you murdered one Jeremiah Cox with a knife that you surrendered as evidence. You pled guilty?"

"Yes," I said. Well, I did do it. Wasn't going to get away from that fact, no matter how much I might want to. I killed a man. A man who deserved it. He'd been leading an army of zombies to destroy my campus, after all. He needed to be put down, or else countless more people would have died.

But he had still been a human. Before him, I'd never killed a human. Killed a lot of things that used to be human. A lot of zombies and ghouls that looked human enough. But they weren't human. And that mattered. I'd killed Jeremiah Cox, a necromancer, and in the eyes of the law, I was a murderer.

"My…a…client," my lawyer began. I couldn't help but wince. Maybe I should talk. Couldn't do much worse.

"I hope this knave has more up his sleeve than a debilitating speech impediment," Treth, the knightly spirit and voice in my head, said. I resisted grinning at the remark. Wouldn't do well for my case, smiling at a murder trial.

"My client," my lawyer repeated, much more fluidly. Perhaps his nerves were finally settling. "Was defending herself against Jerem…Jeremiah Cox. I woul…d… like to remind the court that Mr Cox was a proven necromancer, and responsible for the 21st of April attack on the University of Cape Town. An attack, I m…must remind the court resulted in the deaths of thirty-five people."

Those thirty-five people were also on my conscience. I had made Jeremiah my enemy. He had attacked UCT because of me. To get back at me for destroying his plans. While I could never reasonably blame myself for the actions of monsters, I did feel partly responsible. I always would.

"The actions of Jeremiah Cox are irrelevant to this case," the public prosecutor replied. "Private citizens do not have the right to dispense their version of the law. This is a nation of laws and vigilantes go up against that law. Ms Drummond had no right to take the law into her own hands."

They were perfectly fine when we killed monsters, even the sentient ones, but dare trample on the cops' prerogative of arresting humans and the Reaper have mercy on your soul!

"I must remind the public prosecutor," the magistrate said, "that while vigilantism is illegal, the actions of Jeremiah Cox are relevant to the case at hand."

"Thank...thank you, your honour. Jeremiah's actions are deeply relevant to this case. Not only was he a criminal whose death stopped the massacre on campus, he was also directly threatening the life of Ms Drummond. My client was acting in self-defence, a principle held sacrosanct by the Spirit of the Law."

My lawyer was, of course, referring to the semi-sentient spirit that governed the constitution of Hope City. An elemental being crafted by lawmancy only a few years after the Cataclysm, the event that brought magic and monsters into our world. It kept the City Council in line and set forth an unchangeable set of legal principles to govern the rule of law in the city.

"If you are referring to the threat that Jeremiah's army posed to the campus, then Ms Drummond was within her rights to eliminate the undead but was not within her rights to extend that attack to the necromancer himself. Necromancy may be recognised as dark magic, but its practitioners are still not considered lesser humans. They have the right to a fair trial, and not execution by a wannabe monster hunter."

I clenched my fist but before I could retort, the magistrate did for me.

"Please withdraw that last statement."

"Withdrawn, your honour."

As if it was withdrawn! Sham case. All a sham.

"Your honour," my lawyer said, "I would like to bring my first witness to the stand."

The magistrate nodded and gestured towards the witness stand. I heard the doors open behind me and booted feet thud on the old wooden flooring. I glanced back from my position in the defendant's chair and saw a woman I recognised.

She was in her thirties. Short blonde hair, in a pixie cut. Thick-rimmed glasses. She wore a sleeveless white and blue robe with a caduceus emblazoned on the front. Her arms were scarred with cursive runes. Pranish would probably recognise which primordial tongue it was. I only knew it was one of the good ones. This woman was a healer and purification mage, working in some capacity with Drakenbane, a monster-hunting agency that helped me on campus. She had been there and had used

10

the spell scarring her arms to de-animate a horde of undead. Last time I had seen her, her magical efforts had left her eyes dark and vomit caking her chin and chest.

The healer took a seat at the witness stand and my lawyer approached her.

"Your name, age and profession, please."

"Cindy Giles. 33. Auxiliary-Healer and Purification Specialist for the Drakenbane Agency. Member of the Association of Heiligeslicht."

"Thank you." My lawyer turned towards me and the almost empty courtroom. "Cindy Giles specialises in understanding and eliminating dark magic. In her capacity at Drakenbane, she also acts as a magical forensics specialist. She was present during the 21st of April attacks and studied the scene in Jammie Hall, including the body of Jeremiah Cox. Ms Giles, can you tell the court what you found?"

"Besides the already established necromantic rituals and traces of reanimation spell work in the air, the body of Jeremiah Cox had the unmistakable essence of an unfinished incantation. He was in the process of casting a spell when he died."

"Can you tell what type of spell?"

Cindy nodded. Face serious, but tone calm. She must be used to being at court. As a forensics expert, she'd have to be.

"Amazing that people can do stuff like this," Treth said. "We could have stopped the necromancer cabals decades ago if we could detect their magic."

"The spell was a dark incantation of the corruption variety. It was a high-level decay spell."

"Can you tell the court what this spell would have accomplished if its incantation had been completed, Ms Giles?"

My lawyer was definitely in the swing of things now. He must have grown more confident that he could win this. His stutter was gone, replaced with a subtle but confident grin.

"If the spell was fully cast," Cindy hesitated, looked at me, and then continued. "the victim would have been wracked by internal bleeding, then faced accelerated rotting of the limbs, until their vital organs finally failed, and they died."

The room was silent. My lawyer cleared his throat and then spoke.

"Thank you, Ms Giles. That is all."

Cindy nodded and left the stand. She gave me a small smile as she left the courtroom. Must be a busy lady. I'd need to thank her properly.

I turned to watch Cindy leave and saw two new figures enter. They wore black combat vests; their holsters empty as security would be holding onto their weapons. A picture of a red drake in flight was emblazoned on their vests. Brett and Guy. Drakenbane agents who had helped me during the attack.

"I have two more witnesses to bring to the stand…"

"Enough," the magistrate put up his hand in a motion to halt. "I do not see the need for any additional witnesses, Mr Philips."

That was his name! Colin Philips. A young lawyer who had volunteered to take on my case free of charge. Didn't know much about him. Just knew how nervous he was. But, he was winning this now by the looks of it. If I got out of this thanks to him, I'd also need to thank him. And Brett and Guy. Brett had irritated me in the past, still irritated me, but for him to come out here to help me…

We both owed each other a lot of amorphous favours. We were in that type of work. You indebt yourself with one another so much that when the gates to hell finally open, you knew you'd have each other's back. Brett was obnoxious, but earnest. I'd dare say he was my friend, now.

Colin stood next to me. We all remained silent. The public prosecutor was checking his watch. Another busy person. He probably had a dead rapist to defend after this. A thankless job.

The magistrate scanned the room to ensure no one was speaking out of turn. Not sure why he took the effort. Not many people to look at. Satisfied, he finally spoke.

"The evidence collected is clear and the necessary formal proceedings have been completed. Ms Drummond, the state of Good Hope recognises that your act of self-defence was right and in proportion to the threat levelled against you."

A pause.

"But, as vigilantism is a crime, you will need to surrender a fine of $500 to the court. Court dismissed!"

$500.

The price of a human life.

For Jeremiah Cox's life, I'd have charged a lot lower.

A single bang of the gavel signalled for us to leave. The public prosecutor checked his watch again in a hurried fashion and then approached Colin and me. He offered his hand to Colin and congratulated him on his first case, then he turned to me and offered his hand.

"I'm glad it worked out this way, Ms Drummond," he said, with a smile of ivory white. "Please forgive me for the proceedings. It's my job, after all."

I nodded, understandingly. The public prosecutor left in a hurry and Colin turned to me to shake my hand.

"I guess this is a debt repaid," he said. His stutter was mostly gone.

"Debt?" I asked, but then froze. I remembered. I'd seen Colin before. He had been under attack by two red-jacketed sorcerers. I had saved him, and he'd run off.

"You saved me and my notes. Passed the bar thanks to you."

Slightly embarrassed that he had remembered me, I looked at the floor.

"Just the right time...right place."

"Well, think of this being the same for me. Was at the station visiting a friend when you were brought in. Probably wouldn't have found out you'd been cuffed if I hadn't been there."

"I'm glad you were there then." I smiled.

"Oi, Katty. You smell that?"

I turned to see Brett and Guy. Brett had his hands on his waist and a beam splitting his face in two.

"Smell what?"

Brett took a deep breath, and then exclaimed. "Freedom!"

I chuckled and turned to Guy. "Thanks for coming, both of you."

Guy nodded. "Thank Cindy. Was her testimony that got you freed."

"I will. Definitely. Where is she off to now?"

"Archdemon popped out a rift near Pinelands. She's gone to help sanctify the area before more can show up."

I whistled, impressed. Archdemons were not small fry by any stretch of the imagination. They were beings of pure primordial energy, channelling their power into nefarious deeds. Cindy must have been a very accomplished mage to be called in on an operation against one.

"Well, better be off, Katty. Dragons to slay. See you around!"

"See you." I waved them off and turned back to Colin.

"You have good friends," he said.

"Them? They're not…well, yeah. I do."

"It's more than that, though."

I cocked my head, inquisitively. I was taller than Colin, and he was looking down, fidgeting with the pockets of his shelf-bought suit.

"This was a waste of time case, wasn't it?" he said. The question was rhetorical, but I answered anyway.

"Would have been a bigger waste of time if I'd been convicted." I shrugged.

"That wouldn't happen. You heard Jan, the prosecutor. He didn't really even want to prosecute you. Just his job. The magistrate probably would have let you off regardless."

"Don't underestimate the ineptitude of government," I grinned. "You made them see reason. Reason being that I should walk free, that is. Thanks, again."

Colin smiled. "Was the least I could do. Couldn't have you behind bars for saving my alma mater. If you hadn't done what you did, there'd be many more than just thirty-five dead. Worth defending you for that."

I repressed a wince. If I hadn't done what I did in the first place, there may not be anyone dead at UCT.

"He's right, Kat," Treth said. "Stop kicking yourself over those deaths. You did what you could. You're a hero for that."

Some hero…

"The Drakenbane guys agree with me. They should. They're in the same boat you are. Monster hunters. They understand what needs to be done."

What needs to be done…

Colin shook his head, his cheeks reddening. Not from shyness, but from anger.

"Wouldn't do to have someone behind bars for doing the right thing."

Colin put out his hand again, suddenly, and looked me in the eyes.

"Thanks, Kat. For doing the right thing."

A bit cheesy, ain't it? But, I'm embarrassed to admit - moving. I shook his hand. His grip was weak, but earnest. I looked him in the eyes.

"Thanks, Colin. I really mean it."

He nodded once, a serious look on his face, and then bid me farewell. He had another case after this. A paid one.

The courtroom was all but empty. A security guard was standing at the open doorway, waiting for me to leave. I took a deep breath. Brett was right. It did smell like freedom. I left the room.

Outside, leaning up against the wall beside a coffee machine, was a dark-skinned man with greased back, black hair, a cream suit and pinstripe tie. Conrad Khoi. My agent. Basically, my boss. He didn't look happy.

"So, you're free?"

I nodded. "Just owe the court $500. Should be fine with the bounty on Jeremiah and any other jobs you can get me."

Conrad shook his head. His arms were crossed.

"City reneged on the bounty. We got nothing."

"Shit."

I clenched my fists. I needed that money. Really needed that money now. Really needed to work fast now. I did some mental calculations. Treth helped.

"Could clear that with one or two wights. A zombie mob would also do the trick."

It wasn't a disaster. I could come back from this.

"Then time for me to get back on the job," I said to Conrad. To my surprise, he shook his head.

19

"Nobody is saying it openly, Kat, but we're all thinking it. Your impulsive stunt with Jeremiah caused the attack. If I put you back on the job before public suspicion abated, then I'll be damaging my reputation."

I opened my mouth to respond. Conrad raised his hand to stop me.

"No use arguing, Kat. You fucked up. Fucked up big time. That means you're on hiatus. Just until things blow over."

"How you going to pay your own bills?" I spat. Regretted it.

"Got other freelancers. None, admittedly, as good as you. But at least they don't cause massacres."

That stung. That stung a lot.

Conrad pushed himself off the wall and walked past me.

"I'll have something for you in the next few weeks. Consider this a holiday."

I stood with my fists clenched, facing the wall.

Rent was due, needed to pay for next semester's tuition, needed a full-bodily purification and check-up, and needed to eat.

Some holiday…

Chapter 2. Friends

"You sure you know how to do this?" I asked, a shameful quaver in my voice as I lay on Trudie's cold countertop in her parent's kitchen.

"Do you really need to do it here?" Trudie asked, a slight whine in her voice. All the appliances that used to be on the counter were now lying on the couch.

"You want Ms Grumpy-guts here to continue snapping at us all the time?" Pranish asked, tracing some runes onto a sheet of papyrus.

Trudie grumbled her reply. Her annoyance at her kitchen being turned into a purification ritual site was only surpassed by her irritation at my general demeanour.

Exams had ended a week ago and I'd been a real asshole. Snapping at everyone. Yelling. Whining. Duer, the pixie living in my apartment, had even stopped trying to yell back.

All in all, I had been in a terrible mood. An unnaturally bad mood. Was more than just my financial trouble, the boredom from lack of work and the mounting post-traumatic stress from all my hunts and killing a human.

When you're covered in as much cursed undead blood as I am, you start becoming cursed. Most curses are relatively harmless. They're like bugs. They make you sluggish, light-headed, cranky. As they mount up, they darken your personality. They make your life shit. With all the curses clinging to me, I was making myself very unpleasant to be around. Well, at least I didn't get necro-sick. Didn't feel like vomiting up my intestines just yet.

Because of my increasingly irritable behaviour and inability to pay for a purification, my friend, Pranish, offered to do a purification himself. Pranish was a sorcerer – a magic user with an innate well of magic called the spark. But, he seldom used sorcery. His spark was weak, much to the chagrin of his magicorp family. To make up for his shortcomings, however, Pranish studied wizardry, the art of channelling the magic of the world into incantation and enchantment. By speaking the primordial tongues, wizards could channel the magical circuits of the world – weylines – to accomplish many things.

Pranish had been spending the last hour tracing runes that looked like a cross between Egyptian hieroglyphics and Mesopotamian cuneiform onto a sheet of papyrus. He hadn't ever done a purification before and was painstakingly ensuring every curve of every ancient letter was accurate. Scroll-making and incantation were dangerous, and Pranish had never done this before. A lot could go wrong. One slight mispronunciation, and I could end up glowing pink for the next year. And that was the least of what could happen…

"If we're going to eat before going out, then you need to do this today…" Trudie said, tapping her foot.

"I'd rather he go as slowly as needed," I said, restraining my voice from coming out as a hiss.

"And done," Pranish said, with a flourish of his griffon feather quill. "Make way, proprietor of the house. I have work to do!"

Trudie moved off to the side. She faced away from the counter, but still peeked over her shoulder. Despite her disdain for the arcane and love of technology, she must have had at least some interest.

"You sure he can handle this?" Treth asked, a shiver in his voice. I couldn't blame him. I didn't trust magic at the best of times and, while I trusted Pranish, I didn't necessarily trust his handle on magic.

"Stay still," Pranish said. I felt him sprinkle something on my toes. I looked up.

"Stay still! If you must know, I'm creating a ritual circle out of holy salt."

"What makes it holy?" Trudie asked, her disdain only thinly masking some genuine curiosity.

"Unicorn shit and a Titan priest. Hell if I know! But the stuff is used by the professionals."

Pranish was right. Had salt used on me by a lot by purifiers. They typically used simple incantation though. They didn't need scrolls. Memorised the one spell they needed for their livelihood and could deal with that strain. Pranish couldn't afford to do that. Memorising the primordial tongues was tiring. One too many pyromancy spells and your head could literally explode. But purifiers only needed to know the one spell for their use. For Pranish, he needed to write the spell down and then incant it, while using the runes to channel the spell into a cast.

Finally, Pranish sprinkled some salt on my face. I closed my eyes. Had gotten salt in my eyes once. Wasn't pleasant.

"Comfortable?" Pranish asked.

"Comfortable as I'll ever be," I snarled.

"Good, I'll begin."

He proceeded to start babbling some arcane poppycock. Some pseudo-ancient Egyptian and quasi-Latin. Well, the Egyptian and Latin is what is really the fake. The words of power predate human language. They predate humanity. They were the words of nature itself.

I heard a hiss and the crumpling of paper, as if consumed by fire. But I didn't smell burning. I had seen scrolls used before. They were once-off affairs, disintegrating into golden flame upon use. Wizardry was a time-consuming discipline. It required hours, if not days and weeks, of prep-work, enchanting and memorisation. Sorcerers, on the other hand, only needed to exert their wordless will. Well, they couldn't do anything quite so delicate as a wizard though. Most sorcerers didn't seem to care. I probably wouldn't, either, if I could control the elements.

With a concluding phrase that sounded like honey and butterflies to my ears, I felt a physical weight lift off me. The salt surrounding me and placed on my feet and forehead let out a faint warmth and then disappeared.

"At least we don't need to clean up," Trudie said.

I opened my eyes.

"How do you feel?" Pranish asked. His eyes were anxious. The anxiety of a scientist contemplating his hypothesis.

"Hungry."

He froze.

"Hungry, and better than I've felt in weeks."

He sighed with palpable relief and then beamed. His smile shone almost as much as the gold and ivory necklet that his parents wanted him to wear to aid his spark.

"Well done, Pranish." I smiled. I really did feel better. Had never had that many curses on me before. Having them off me, I felt giddy with purity.

"So, you ready to decide what we're going to do tonight?" Trudie asked as I got off the countertop and straightened my ruffled t-shirt and denim jeans.

"Was always ready to decide."

Trudie rolled her eyes. "You were hissing up a storm. Couldn't get anything other than curses out of you."

"And now the curses are out," I grinned. "And thus, we can proceed."

"Proceed where?" I heard a voice ask. Andy Garce, IT major alongside Pranish and Trudie, was leaning up against the doorframe leading towards the front door.

"Andy?!" Trudie said, a look of complete confusion upon her face. "How'd you get in?"

Andy was expected, so Trudie's greeting was not meant to come off as rude. But I was also curious how he entered the house without Trudie letting him in.

"You left the door unlocked." Andy grinned, that confident and likeably cocky grin of his.

Trudie looked even more quizzical, and a bit flustered underneath all her white and black bubble-goth make-up.

"I was sure…" she started muttering, and then stopped. "Well, now that you're here, you can join the vote. We're deciding how to spend such an illustrious evening."

"What makes it illustrious?"

"I'm finally in a good mood," I said.

"No more curses?"

"None that are of any consequence."

"I got them all, Kat. You're clean for at least another few minutes," Pranish said, wiping excess salt off his hands with a napkin.

"Well," Andy said, looking at me as I put my shoes back on. "Good to have you back on the side of the good and righteous."

"Never left. Just feeling a bit less misanthropic. Now, let's get to discussing these plans before Trudie throws a fit."

Trudie rolled her eyes but appreciated me moving on with the discussion all the same.

"So, here's my idea," she said, rubbing her hands together as if announcing a cunning scheme. "We head into Old Town, go past the Night Market and pick up some food, and then we head to the Eternity Lounge for some sweet tunes and dancing."

I winced. Trudie and I had been friends for practically forever, but that didn't mean our interests aligned that well. I was all for the night market and eating. Food is great, after all. Especially street food. But dancing and tunes, in a cacophonous enclosed space filled with cigarette smoke…

That wasn't my idea of fun. My job was about managing chaos, dealing with acrid stench and tolerating loud noises. I didn't want to go to a place reminiscent of a battleground for fun.

Pranish shrugged. I knew he didn't like the Eternity Lounge either. Too many people. We liked Trudie, but only one of her. Last time we all went to the lounge, I was honestly sure there were at least three vampire punks there.

Trudie glanced from Pranish, to me. I squirmed, thinking of any sort of excuse why I needed to be home. Then, Andy came to the rescue.

"Not a fan of clubs, myself. Would prefer something quieter, where we can talk."

Andy went up my list of people I like ten-fold.

Trudie, starting to look a bit worried that her plan was going to fail, turned to Pranish. I looked at him too. He pretended to not notice our gazes as he packed up his wizardry equipment.

"Pranish, club or no club?" Trudie asked.

"Hmmm…" Pranish pretended to contemplate the question. "To be honest, I'd prefer to go to one place. So, a place where we can eat, and then hang out."

I felt almost sorry for Trudie. Only almost. She could go to the Eternity Lounge on her own time.

"Howabout the Gravekeeper?" I suggested, the words out of my mouth before I could think. But then again, it was a good place to go. The kitchen always smelled nice when I walked past on the way to see Conrad. A pub was always preferable to a club. Had food, open windows, cheaper drinks and a tolerable level of noise.

Trudie frowned. "That pub in Obz?"

I nodded.

"The one where your creepy boss has his office?"

I dismissed the comment with a wave of my hand. "I'm on vacation, so he's not my boss. And besides, they've got good food and plenty of affordable drinks. And if you're smashed enough, you won't need a dancefloor."

Trudie sighed, resigned. "Okay. Have it your way. We'll go to the Gravekeeper. I'm sure after a few beers I'll start thinking it's the Eternity Lounge."

***

Trudie was a famous lightweight. She wasn't joking when she said she'd just need a few beers. After about 2 pints, she was almost comatose.

The four (five, if you include Treth) of us were sitting in a corner booth of the Gravekeeper tavern. Glistening golden pints of ale and beer dripped streams of condensation onto the dark, hardwood table. While there was the putrid stench of cigarette smoke rising from Trudie's ashtray, it was overpowered by the rich aroma of pulled pork and golden fries. I managed to wake up Trudie long enough for her to eat her meal before she fell asleep at her seat again. I glanced her way throughout the evening. She was so peaceful and cute while asleep. No semblance of the moodiness that I loved and tolerated in her. Just an even more lovable vulnerability in her peaceful, liquor-induced exhaustion.

Andy loved the Gravekeeper. Said it was his type of joint. Pranish, while concerned with some runes, also voiced his mild admiration of the place.

It was a pleasant evening among friends, filled with light conversation. By light, I of course mean of the highest intellectual calibre and controversy. No space for small talk here. Pranish and Andy had an argument over the differences between sprites and pixies and expected me to judge who was right. I tried my best, indicating that while both are fae, sprites tend to be more linked to nature than pixies. But, admittedly, I don't know much about fae. I wonder what Duer would have thought of it all? I should ask him. I may never fight a fae, if I can help it, but it is always good to learn about these creatures we now share our planet with.

The argument was good natured, though, if heated. It moved on to Warpwars, which we were all fans of, and then onto complaining about the general politics of the campus.

Eventually, early evening turned to late-night. The chatter of the early drinking crowd was replaced with the more drunken babble of those who remained and pub crawlers from around Hope City. I was pacing myself drinks-wise. Sure, I can have fun. But fun was no excuse to be non *compos mentis*. What if a gül burst into the pub? I had my swords with me (never left home without them any more) but needed a clear head to use them.

Pranish, finishing up his fifth gin and tonic, checked his smart watch and showed an expression of complete disgust. Andy was rattling off about something that happened during lectures, but I was now paying attention to my friend as he stood up and retrieved his jacket.

"What's up?" I asked.

"Brother needs some work done."

"That prick?"

"Yes, that prick." Pranish winced. "Well, I'll be seeing you. Kat, Andy. Trudie, if you can hear me in dreamland."

Pranish departed soon after, leaving just the three of us. A comatose goth girl. A monster hunter on her break. And some guy. Well, not just any guy. I liked Andy. I really did. He was fun and easy to talk to. But that didn't mean I wanted to be basically alone with him. At least, not yet.

An awkward silence fell over the table. I swirled my ale and then took a drink. It wasn't as cold any more. The cost of prudent drinking. If only I could be as impulsive with my drinks as I was with my hunts.

"So…" Andy said. The awkwardness thickened.

"So…" I parroted.

"Don't do this to me, Kat," Treth said, desperation in his voice. "I'm feeling awkward now."

I had gotten used to the voice in my head and had become adept at not making it register that he had spoken.

34

Andy would, hopefully, not even see a facial twitch. He was looking at me awfully closely though. I averted my gaze, pretending to study the texture of the table, but I couldn't help but notice that he had amber eyes.

"Kat..." he started. His tone sounded serious, sincere. Something heavy.

"Kat!" a voice interrupted him. Both our heads swivelled at once. Conrad, wearing a purple suit without a tie, with bedraggled hair and bags under his eyes, came right up to the table. He spared a slight quizzical glance at Trudie, and none for Andy.

"Got a job for you."

"Hi, Conrad. This is Andy."

Andy stood and put out his hand. Conrad didn't shift his gaze, ignoring Andy's offer. Andy sat down again, his expression unchanged.

"Details in my office."

"It's..." I checked the time on my phone. "11pm. Really time for business?"

"Been out of the game that long? This is business hours."

I sighed and stood up.

"I better take this, Andy. Nice hanging out."

"Same, Kat. I'll make sure Trudie gets home safe."

"Pfft. She can handle herself, but thanks." I smiled, and then followed Conrad up to his too-small office.

It was messier than I remembered. Documents of various languages and runes covered every surface, some sticking out of folders like a bouquet of flowers.

"Been busy?" I chided.

"After your stunt, I had to keep busy."

"I could have helped."

I picked up a document. City Council wanted to investigate a possible lesser vampire beast skulking near Old Town. There was a red cross over the text.

Conrad took a seat. He didn't offer me anything to drink. I would have appreciated a coffee. Was getting a bit faint headed. I could handle my drink, but any amount of alcohol would have an effect on someone.

I took a seat on a pile of already damaged documents. They had red all over them, so I presumed they were no longer important.

"Got an investigation for you to handle."

I winced. "Even after the last time?"

"Even you can't fuck up this one."

He passed me a document. It was a jointly funded case. Monster hunting could get expensive and the Council didn't always feel the need to fund the elimination out of the city budget. In cases like this, people banded together to pay for a hunter.

The document contained a list of cases. Disappearances. Men and women disappearing, all in the same district of Old Town. There were a lot of disappearances in Hope City. A lot of monsters, a lot of criminals. Human traffickers, vampires, necromancers...and rarely, a rift opening and sucking a human into it rather than spitting out its own monster.

"And this..." Conrad said, handing me another page.

Mimic.

I almost laughed out loud.

"They think it's a mimic? Seriously?"

Conrad nodded, face still serious. He looked tired. No amusement.

Mimics were beasts from some medieval world that survived on luring in prey and then consuming them. To accomplish this, they typically disguised themselves as treasure chests, overflowing with gold. The problem for them: nobody fell for it on Earth. If you were going through a computer store, looking for the next Uhurutech gadget, and you saw a wooden and iron chest filled with cartoony treasure, would you think:

"Oh, swell! Treasure. Nothing unusual or dangerous could happen to me now. I'm rich!"

Or:

"Yeah, I'd rather not be eaten by an under-evolved and stupid creature that thinks humanity is still in the dark ages."

You might not think either, but for most humans on post-Cataclysmic Earth, avoiding suspicious treasure became something you learnt from birth. Deaths by mimic were rarer than deaths by pixies. And despite what Duer may tell you, pixies were not that good at killing.

"Seven people," Conrad said, his fingers steepled and his elbows on his desk. "All gone missing in the same area."

"But why a mimic?"

Conrad shrugged. "That's what a private investigator one of the victim's wives hired suggested. He then referred the case over to us."

"Did he give a reason he thought it was a mimic?"

"Read the doc. Says that the kidnappings are too stealthy. Any sort of other creature or human would be seen by someone or detected by magic. He found nothing. No trace of dark magic. Mimics, as you well know, do not emit any sort of magical signature. So, if there're attacks being made, they are being made by something that can cloak its activities."

"Could be an adept mage using non-dark magic to incapacitate their victims and then move them to another area," Treth offered. I said as such to Conrad.

"That's up to you to find out."

He stood up.

"Time to prove yourself again, Kat. If you can put this case to rest and get us a paycheque, then I can put you back on the regular payroll."

I stood up and turned to leave.

"Good luck," Conrad said, as I opened the door. I froze, and then left.

Andy and Trudie were gone and the pub was winding down. Would need to get home and get rested. Vacation was over.

Chapter 3.   Investigation

The sea has a weird smell. On one hand, it is fresh, clean and relaxing. Its salty scent sanitises the air, travelling with the winds to clean the stench it passes along the way. But on the other hand, the sea does not smell clean. It smells of decay. And that should be expected. Think about all the death on land. That's just a fraction of Earth's deaths. Even before the Cataclysm, the oceans took up most of Earth's activities. Every fish birth, life and death, across countless fathoms, depths and swathes of salty water. Post-Cataclysm, the sea had even more things to live and die. Creatures from other worlds. Some mundane. Just fish from worlds similar to our own. Others were much more fantastical. Leviathans, krakens, merfolk and countless more. Modern day humans couldn't begin to fathom post-Cataclysmic Earth. Understanding all there was to understand about the oceans…impossible.

I comment about the sea for good reason. My investigation into the disappearances, apparently at the hands of a mimic, brought me to the Waterfront of Old Town. It was an old area, kept clean and well maintained to impress tourists. The old colonial facades of many buildings were still maintained, kept a clean white. The owners of the buildings profited from having a decent looking city, so they kept their buildings spick and span. The initial settlement in the area, when it was still called Cape Town, had been established nearby. In ages past, this dockyard had serviced military vessels in both World Wars and many more wars before it.

It was an historic district and it piqued my interest as a student of history. But I wasn't here to study old Dutch and English architecture. I was here to investigate the disappearances of seven people, allegedly at the hands of a creature I didn't think was capable of successfully slaying anything other than small animals and unattended children.

I now waited by one of the many quays of Hope City's waterfront, envying smokers for their permanent and all-consuming pastime. I didn't like cigarettes but at least smokers were always occupied. A sea-borne salty and chilly wind assaulted me, but at least I was amply dressed. I was wearing my thick denim jeans, a fur-lined black leather jacket and a red scarf. My swords and equipment were in my bag, by my side. A policeman had looked at the hilts askance, but there was no law against carrying them around. The tick would need to chill.

I was to meet the private investigator. The one who claimed a mimic had eaten the disappearing husbands and wives of the now joint-case clients. Conrad had arranged the meet. At least he was still helping me with something. I had a lot of questions to ask. I wasn't a detective. Wasn't my job to investigate. It was my job to track things down, but you couldn't track a mimic. Typically, you didn't have to. You just looked for the cartoon chest and shot it a few times. But this case was shaping up to be very different from my usual fare.

"What do you think, Treth?" I asked, leaning on a thick metal chain draped across some concrete posts, looking down into the briny depths. There was no one in earshot to think me a tad loony. I was the only one who could hear Treth, after all.

"About the case?"

"Yep. Ever heard of a mimic being effective?"

"They aren't from my world, but from what I've learnt through you, they seem potentially very dangerous. Greed is an effective motivator. And a dangerous vice."

"Also keeps the world going around…"

Treth snorted. Seemed he disagreed. We had very different views on money. I scrimped and saved, earning buck by buck to attain some measure of financial security, and he lived inside my head without any needs or care in the world. He continued.

"People have done much worse than approach a potentially fake treasure chest in the pursuit of wealth. I am surprised mimics don't kill more people."

"Mimics are stupid," I replied. "They must've evolved over the course of generations on their world to disguise themselves as what that world saw as wealth. On Earth? We aren't so enamoured with wooden chests overflowing with gold."

"Shouldn't underestimate human stupidity."

I chuckled in agreement. "Of course. But, en masse, people aren't that stupid. But let's find out…"

I trailed off as I saw an anxious, mousy woman approach me. I raised my eyebrow. Didn't look like a private investigator. The woman was shorter than me, by quite a margin. If not for her worry lines, I'd have thought her a child. She wore small, round glasses and had short, black hair with greying tips. She wore a black buttoned up jacket. I don't know what else I expected? A guy named after a German city wearing a trench coat?

"Kat Drummond?" she asked.

I nodded and presented my hand. She shook it, weakly and shakily. She seemed to be suffering from a lot of anxiety. Too much. Not private investigator material.

"And you must be the PI?"

The woman's eyes widened, like she'd just seen a wraith. She shook her head, wildly.

"No, um. No, no. That's…he…Drake disappeared."

"Drake being the PI?"

"Yes. He…he disappeared last night. Wanted a final look at the area where Piet, my husband, disappeared."

"So, who might you be?"

"I'm Natalie. Victim's wife. One of the victims' wife. There are a lot of us."

I motioned for Natalie to sit down at a nearby bench. She did so, and I stood opposite her, leaning against the thick chain fence.

"She's shaken, Kat. Be nice," Treth reminded me. Since when was I not nice? I ignored him and spoke, keeping a calm and neutral tone.

45

"Tell me what you know, Natalie."

She put her gloved hands between her knees, either to keep warm or to stop them from shaking. Her face was pale. Her eyes were puffy underneath her librarian glasses.

"Piet left for work three weeks ago…he works by the warehouses. Does…foreman work for Shard Industries."

I knew the company. Pranish's family owned it. They were a pretty big deal. Manufactured all sorts of magic products, from spark enhancers to DIY enchantment attachments for cars to make them impervious to bird shit.

"He went to work…on…Monday. Didn't take the car. He walks there. We live nearby. But he didn't come home…"

Her voice cracked a bit, but this sounded practiced. She had repeated this a lot. First to City Council cops, probably, and then many times after. I pitied this woman, who had to go over her trauma again and again, but also felt a much more professional, if misanthropic emotion: irritation that she wasn't getting to the point.

Treth must have somehow read my mind, as he said. "Patience, Kat."

"I went looking for him," she continued. "But nobody had seen him. He didn't arrive at work."

She looked me in the eyes. I almost flinched.

"That isn't like him. He always went to work. Always showed up on time. Always came home on time. He never strayed. Never went out drinking. Never did anything without telling me first."

I nodded, placating her with my agreement.

"I went to look for him but found nothing. But spouses and partners of the people at the warehouse said that their husbands and boyfriends had also gone missing. No trace."

"So, you hired an investigator?"

Natalie nodded. "Cops started an investigation, but you know how it is. They can't get anything done. We hired Drake to look into it. Pooled our money together."

"And he said it was a mimic?"

My tone must have held a hint of disbelief, as she looked up at me, eyes pleading.

"I know it sounds crazy, but Drake was serious. He was a good PI. He was certain it was a mimic. Couldn't find any trace of magic and any non-magical creature would have been noticed. Drake was convinced it was a mimic...but he knew the hunters we hired wouldn't believe him. So, he went looking for it..."

"And then he never came back?"

Natalie gulped, and nodded. I sighed. Sounds like Drake took their money and ran. Scumbag. There were hundreds of these opportunistic bastards looking for a quick buck from the desperate. Probably wasn't a mimic at all. Drake just said the first monster that popped into his head.

"Where did Drake say the *mimic* was?"

"Nearby. In between the warehouse where Piet worked and the Waterfront mall."

"Thanks, Natalie."

I turned to walk away and felt her grab the back of my jacket.

"Please find the creature that did this, Kat."

Natalie wasn't shaking any more. Her eyes were intense. No tears. No tears any more.

I didn't even know if there was a creature to find. I couldn't promise anything. How could I? I had no real leads. Just some scummy PI that had run off with all these peoples' money. But Natalie's gaze…

"I will, Natalie. And I'll kill it."

Natalie let go, and I left towards the area where the supposed mimic had eaten its victims without leaving any trace.

"What do you think, Treth?" I asked, out of earshot of Natalie or anyone else. The cold sea breeze felt somehow ominous on my bare skin. The clouds were darkening.

"Something took those people. Killed them, abducted them…doesn't matter."

"Or, they ran off. The victims sounded like they knew each other. Could have had some pact to all simultaneously divorce their partners."

"Could be. Or could be something much more sinister."

I sighed. The warehouses were ahead. Old face-brick. Much uglier than the colonial era buildings. I felt a bit of pity for Piet, who would have worked in one.

"This isn't my type of case, Treth."

"Why? You track creatures all the time. This is similar."

"Let's say this is a mimic: how am I supposed to track something without feet? And that's if it is even a mimic."

"You've fought unknown monsters before."

"But I've always known roughly where they are, and at least what they're capable of. This Drake did a real disservice to that woman, and to me. I'm going in completely blind."

I sighed again, more heavily than I had done in ages.

"I'm not a detective. I stab things. And this is shaping up to be a real detective job."

I felt Treth open his mouth to try and encourage me, or reprimand me for pessimism, but he said nothing. He probably agreed with me. This wasn't our forte. Wasn't our type of case. I just hoped that Conrad would put us on a real job soon.

Chapter 4.   Pixies

There was no trace of anything unusual in the brick and concrete jungle of warehouses between the Waterfront mall and Piet's place of work. No blood. No body parts. No police tape. No damage from anything but careless ill-repair. It was just a normal industrial zone on a coastline. Normal even by pre-Cataclysm standards. As such, I became less and less convinced that there was a mimic, or even justification for a monster hunt at all. After spending the entire day searching the area for absolutely nothing, I gave up. I'm not a detective. This is not my job. If people have gone missing, it is a private investigator's job, or the police if they could get off their state-subsidized arses.

I told Conrad all this, and he told me to get back to work. I did not. There was no work to get back to. No mimic to slay. No leads to follow. No tracks to, well, track. This wasn't my type of job.

So, I gambled. I bet on my dwindling savings that Conrad would cave first and put me on a real job. In the meanwhile, I continued my holiday.

"Where you off to, Kat?" Duer squeaked. Alex, my black and white tuxedo cat, was circling underneath him.

Duer still insisted that he patrol my apartment, despite the feline hunter below him. He wasn't content to stay in the birdhouse I had bought him and hung in the corner of the room (Trudie had found that a particularly odd addition. She thought my saying it was for a pixie was a joke).

"Off to help Pranish with some wizardry stuff."

"Your cryomancer friend?"

"He'd prefer to be called an enchanter, or a wizard. Not proud of his sorcerous ways."

Duer shrugged and swooped down to the kitchen counter to retrieve some honey, just before Alex jumped up to stop him. Duer flew up to my shoulder.

"Can I come?"

"Thought you didn't like to leave your domain."

"I need a change of scenery."

I paused to contemplate Duer's request. Pixies weren't considered too much of an oddity, and I could defend him from any fae catchers. Couldn't hurt.

"Ow!" I cried out. Alex was clawing up my leg to get to Duer.

I shooed Alex away and Duer flew up and settled on the rim of his birdhouse.

I rubbed the patch of shredded denim. A wonder I thought they were good enough to handle ghouls.

"Fine, Duer. You can come."

Duer jumped up with some palpable level of excitement and did a little jig.

"Hide in my bag first. Then I can explain your existence to Pranish."

I swung my bag onto my back and the pixie flew into its front pouch, his little head poking out.

"You sure it'll be fine?" Treth asked.

"Duer isn't my little secret, Treth."

"Talking to yourself again, Maddy?"

I sighed. I had attempted to explain Treth's existence to Duer many times before. The pixie either chose to ignore me or just didn't understand. Or chose to not understand. Pixies were mischievous little things, and it was in their nature to be annoying. For this reason, more than any other, I tended to cut Duer some slack. He couldn't help who he was, and it wasn't like he was a real threat to anyone.

Duer kept himself hidden among some crumpled-up notes and pens as we walked past Mrs Ndlovu, my landlady. She was a kindly lady, but extremely paranoid. She was convinced that my apartment block was haunted by a wraith, a spirit formed from the essence of the dead's hatred. That wasn't what she was afraid of, though. Mrs Ndlovu was completely fine living in a building that she was convinced was the hunting ground of a dangerous spirit but was terrified that the existence of said spirit may result in her facing legal trouble. To prevent any such lawsuits, Mrs Ndlovu plastered the entire building with disclaimers and warnings about the wraith.

I had been living in this apartment for well over a year and hadn't ever seen a wraith on the premises. Never actually seen a wraith. Knew plenty about them, part of the vocation, but my specialty was hunting the undead. Dealt with a few spirits before, but wraith hunting is something I am definitely not equipped for. Would need a silver sword, first of all, and that was well out of my budget.

"How often did you get out?" I asked Duer, out of earshot of any curious bystanders, as we walked up the residential streets of Old Rondebosch, a relatively well-off neighbourhood in the urban sprawl of Hope City. I didn't want to attract any untoward attention. While pixies weren't exactly an undesirable species, such as the undead or demons, they weren't completely safe either. In fact, they were so desirable a species, that fae hunters thrived off capturing the creatures and selling their body parts to alchemists and mages. I could fend off a fae hunter, but best not attract such attention if I could help it.

"Get out?" he said, his squeak muffled by the layers of material, paper and debris.

"You know? Leave that abandoned house. Couldn't have been pleasant living 24/7 with that terror."

I shuddered just remembering it. The spirit had been much stronger than I expected. While I did manage to exorcise it (somehow), I almost died.

"That was a dirty weyline," he said, matter of factly. "Couldn't just up and leave."

"Oh? So, you never left?"

I was rounding up the corner of my tree-flanked street. On the right, the usual cardboard in the window of the long-closed shop had been taken down. Inside, I saw paint cans and a ladder.

"Oh, new tenants? I hope it's food." My stomach grumbled. "I hope Pranish has some food with him."

Duer hadn't responded. I pressed. "What did you do before you moved into that old house?"

A pause, and then a sigh. A faint, childlike sigh, but somehow bearing the weight of age. I didn't share the well-shaded pavement with anyone else, so if Duer was to speak, we would have plenty of time without drawing undue attention.

"Okay, Kat," he squeaked. "I'll tell you, but there better be honey in it for me."

"And vodka. A trade is a trade."

Silence. Duer must be grinning ear to ear.

"So, tell me your story, Duer."

"Not all of it. But you shall get some of it. The part of the story when I went into the light and came out into darkness."

"Very ominous."

"Ssshhh," Treth shushed me. "I'd like to hear the story."

"I came from a world bristling with life, with crystalline rivers, oceans of green forests and meadows peppered with flowers more splendid than any gem. Underneath the shade of these forests were sturdy mushrooms and fungi to build cities. And towering above, mountains of blue and white. This valley was my home, and the home of many pixies like me. Unlike the humans and elves that we often saw fight amongst themselves, pixie-kind never fought pixie-kind. We didn't need to. We had our places to protect, honey in our larders and lovers to court. But…"

Duer had been speaking in his usual sing-song, cheery lilt, but near the end, his tone sobered.

"The peace ended," he said, as simply and as matter of factly as I had ever heard him speak. "It ended and then came darkness. The meadows died. The trees came next, withering like a carcass in the sun. Every leaf, blackened. They didn't even fall to the ground. They just turned black and fell apart. Like ash, in the wind. And then, the white and blue mountains became dark. Evil…evil had come…"

Duer stopped speaking, as I heard a quaver in his voice. I whispered.

"You can talk about it another time."

"And miss out on honey?" he tried to make it sound joking. Failed.

"I'll get you honey regardless. You've been keeping the apartment clean, after all."

"It's fine…I can keep going. A promise is a promise. As I was saying, evil came to the valley. My home. Pixies are not a warlike people, but we learn quickly. And we can be bloodthirsty blighters when we want to be. When monsters descended on my people, I came to their defence. I kissed my wife and baby son goodbye, and I flew to war."

"You have a family?"

"Had."

"I'm sorry."

"Don't get me wrong. I don't know if they're dead. Hopefully, the elves and humans put aside their differences long enough to come to our defence. Hopefully. But they aren't my family any more. How can they be? We are no longer of the same world. It has been too long."

"They never stop being your family, Duer."

"For all that's worth," Treth added, a sombre tone.

"I flew with my banner lord to the Peak of Gr'edo," he continued. "As I said, we pixies are not a warlike people. We had no swords, no battle-magic, no war machines. But we had heart. And a will to fight for our lives and families."

"Very noble, Duer."

"Thanks, Kat. And I hope that nobility was enough."

I raised my eyebrow. Duer stopped speaking as we heard footsteps. A man wearing ripped, stained clothes trudged past, scratching his back. Once he was gone, I spoke up.

"What do you mean? What happened at the battle?"

A pause and then. "I don't know."

"How?" I asked, simply, and regretted my tone. But I was curious. I wanted to know how this story ended.

"A warlock, covered in dark purple and black, lifted his hand as me and my kin charged their lines. Then all I saw was light. And then, night. Night underneath a cloudy sky, between cold, hard mountains, covered in glass."

"Earth?"

Duer's silence was affirmation enough.

At least, I thought so. And then I noticed the weight of my backpack lessen by the weight of a single pixie and a bunch of almost forgotten history notes. I spun on my heels to the sight of a man's back. The man from earlier, with the ragged clothing. He was running.

If I've learnt anything from my time as a monster hunter, it is to chase anything that runs away.

I shot off, sneakers beating the pavement. Didn't need to stop to draw my swords. I still felt their weight in my bag, though. The man had just taken Duer. A fae catcher, probably. Bastard. Wouldn't need them, though. Had killed enough people already this year.

And…

I pulled the man's long, greasy hair back, knocking him off balance, and then I ploughed my elbow into his face. His nose caved, and he dropped. I kicked him again to make sure he would stay down.

…I don't need swords for scum like this.

He was wearing a brown, ripped up canvas jacket, bulging with all sorts of knick-knacks. My hand felt slimy after touching his hair. Milk and crumbs stained his beard.

Do I really have to touch him again? I grimaced and wrinkled my nose. He smelled like booze. Bad booze. I heard a squeak.

"Well, here I go."

I squatted to rifle through his things. Didn't feel guilty about it. If someone's gonna go through my stuff, I got the right to go through theirs. But it was unpleasant nonetheless. Didn't like touching grossly unhygienic people at the best of times.

I hope this is not what Trudie thinks of me after a hunt and a lack of shower.

"Kat?" I heard a squeak. Sounded more curious than frightened.

"I'm here. I opened the jacket. A lot of shit. I wrestled through clutter, pulling things out, until I saw Duer cramped into a small jam jar, nail sized holes in the lid. I opened it up.

"Sorry, Kat. He put some jinx on me. Couldn't speak…" Duer trailed off. He was hovering over the jar, staring at the ground. I looked down, at the fae catcher's things. Corpses. Wings. Dried tiny little bodies. Miniature children's bodies, with their wings snipped off, nails through their hearts. Some missing limbs. A cheese grater, stained red, gold and black.

I felt like I was going to get sick. I covered my mouth. Shock, and to stop myself from dirtying the comatose man even further with my own innards.

"I didn't finish the story," Duer said, in a voice sadder than I had ever heard from him before.

He floated up onto my shoulder. He couldn't go into my bag. The fae catcher bastard had cut open the front pocket.

"I wasn't the only one to arrive on Earth, among your forests of plastic, glass and concrete. There were many of us once. It wasn't my family, but they became like my family. Other pixies from the valley. From my battalion…"

Duer stared intently at the pixie corpses on the pavement. I'm not sure if at any in particular. But I got the feeling he saw different faces on those corpses than I. Faces of friends. Faces of neighbours. Faces of family, long lost. Duer claimed he had given up going back to his home. That he had somehow moved on from his family. But nobody ever forgot their family. Nobody ever moved on.

Duer opened his mouth to speak but closed it again. He didn't need to say any more. I understood.

Fae catchers weren't considered criminals, and pixie bits fetched a high price on the market. Everyone from alchemists looking for reagents and impotence sufferers looking for something to grant them manliness sacrificed these little winged people for their own gain. I had never seen a dead pixie before, but I had learnt about pixie-related narcotics in school. The real thing was worse than the fear-mongering classes.

Duer had not arrived on Earth alone. But he was now. That meant he had survived a lot. Too much for any one person his size to survive. But he had, and that had left him alone. Alone to fend for himself in a big world, full of blinking lights, loud noises and scum that wanted to snort his ground down bones.

I clenched my fist and considered ending this fae catcher's miserable and stinking existence. But I had taken too many lives already. Instead, I opened up his jacket, and took all his loot. Every last corpse, every last pixie related drug, powder, dust, bonemeal and pinned wings. I collected them into his jacket and used it as a bag. I must admit, I also took all his money. For the inconvenience, and to buy myself a new backpack. Consider it payment for services rendered. Don't ask me on the behalf of whom.

Duer didn't ask what I was doing with the pixie bits. I had a feeling he knew already. I was going to be late to help Pranish, but this was more important.

I took a footpath down towards the canal, near Riverstone Mall. It had been raining recently, and the water flowed freely, washing away dirt and litter from the canal. Lilies, flowers and shrubbery grew within and around the waterway. Trees grew over it, forming a shade that separated this portion of the Liesbeeck from the outside world. I stopped, breathed in the fresh air. I couldn't smell any fumes, or people. Just nature. Water and plants.

A river below me. It wasn't crystalline, but it was close enough. Trees. A few of them. A forest by some stretch of the imagination. And some flowers. They were pretty. I am not sure if as pretty as Duer's *gems*, but I liked them. Lastly, I turned and looked at Table Mountain, the tomb of the titan Adamastor. In this light, the splendid mountain could be seen as blue.

"Are pixies buried? How do you send off your people?"

Duer nodded. "We bury them, so they can be reclaimed by the soil."

I nodded and placed the fae catcher's jacket on the ground. I began digging with my bare hands. The soil was soft. Moist. A hole formed easily. Big enough for all the minute bodies of Duer's kind.

I placed each pixie side by side, when possible. Some were just bits. An arm. A wing. A tunic. But I gave each bit a portion of this unmarked grave and wondered if there was any more I could do.

Duer looked into the grave, or beyond it. I filled the hole and placed a single daisy on top of the mound.

And then Duer sang. A song that sent tingles down my spine. It was sad, but not the type of sad that makes you cry. It was too sorrow-filled for crying. And while I could not understand the words, I felt them. But how can I explain them? They spoke to me, and what I have lost, and for what I will lose in the future. It reminded me that I will lose again. And again, and again. But it also reminded me that there was more. More than loss. Because there's always a light at the end of the tunnel. And that light is worth the darkness.

Duer flew up into my jacket pocket and we left. None of us spoke for the remainder of the journey. Not me, Duer, or Treth.

Chapter 5.   Family

"Unlike you to be late, Kat," Pranish said, opening the door with his usual grin. He frowned for a second at the pixie perched on the rim of my jacket pocket but didn't ask about it yet. Pranish was used to the abnormal – especially when it came to me. I entered his apartment, nestled in Old Rondebosch like mine. But, admittedly, in a much better part of Old Rondebosch.

While my apartment was dank and dark, under the shadow of a skyscraper, Pranish's was sunny, with open windows letting in fresh air. On top of that, while my apartment was messy, strewn with food wrappers and study notes, Pranish's was spotless. All his books and notes were neatly filed and stored away in a multitude of shelves, colour coded. Pranish was a stickler for systems. Don't let his cheery and off-hand demeanour deceive you. Pranish has a stick up his arse longer than a leviathan. Still my friend, though.

I made my way into Pranish's living room, clean and as modern as the rest of the house. A glass-top coffee table dominated the centre of a maroon rug, flanked by a leather couch and armchair. Pranish, at first glance, was pretty well off for someone who worked part-time retail. But his parents were bigwig sorcerous executives, after all. He was already a shame to them for his lack of innate magical energy. They didn't want him tarnishing the family name by exhibiting poverty now, did they?

"So," Pranish said, taking a seat opposite me as I slumped down onto the couch, spreading my arms across the back. Right at home.

Pranish glanced at Duer, who stared back at him.

"Are you going to introduce us?"

"Pranish," I indicated Duer in my jacket pocket. "Meet Duer. Duer, Pranish."

"Nice to meet you, Duer." Pranish leant forward with his hand outstretched. Duer stared at it for a bit and then put out his own. Pranish shook, gently. Was like watching someone grasping a needle with their fist.

"So, how did you get a hold of a pixie?"

"He more got a hold of me. Moved in to my apartment after that haunting a few months back."

"Kat destroyed my home."

"Shush. The terror destroyed his, and its, home. So, he moved in with me."

67

"Good move. Pixies are stellar weyline purifiers."

"Oh! So, he wasn't lying."

Duer glanced at me, dismay and anger seeping cloyingly off his face. I patted him on his tiny head.

"I still let you stay, didn't I?"

"Well," Pranish said, rubbing his hands together. "No more delays. Let's get started."

"What is it exactly that you need?" I asked. I'd agreed to come help, but Pranish was usually very vague in everything he did. Overly excitable. Forgot that others weren't privy to his thoughts.

Pranish stopped, looked a bit lost and then said, "Oh yeah. Nothing serious. Not a test subject or anything. Just need you to help me replicate some scrolls."

"I ain't a wizard, Prani."

"That was almost a reference," Pranish grinned. "But don't worry. You don't need to strain your already strained mind with any arcana. I'll be doing all the channelling. Just need you to help me write down the runes."

"With my handwriting? Rest in peace to whoever uses these scrolls."

"Hopefully not. You'll be the one using them."

I raised my eyebrow at that.

"I'm testing out some activated enchantments – scrolls that can be used on the fly. Much safer than memorising spells and much less energy intensive than permanent enchantments. But, I need someone to test it."

"Thought you said I wasn't going to be the test subject."

"Not testing them on you, but I'd like you to test them."

"Sounds to me like I'm a test subject."

Pranish's grin split his face in two. "Well, are you in?"

I sighed. I wasn't sure about it, but Pranish was my friend.

"Sure, show me what to do."

Pranish guided me to his dining room, dominated by another glass table top. Markers and thin cardboard sheets were neatly piled on the surface. Always the stickler for organisation. Well, I could learn a thing or two from him.

Pranish showed me some scrolls he had already drawn and then indicated how to draw them myself. Runemancy was a delicate discipline. I couldn't just scribble down the symbols on a sheet. I needed to do them in the right order.

Every curve, corner and serif had to be completely accurate. I must admit, the endeavour did have me a bit stressed. One wrong pixel and a scroll of hardening could turn into a liquification curse. Well, not that bad. But I'm a bit paranoid about magic. Gives me the creeps. And as I constantly remind you, I hunt horror for a living.

I had gone through enough scrolls to barely satisfy Pranish when the doorbell rang. Pranish, who had been humming contentedly, stopped, and paled. His one eye was glowing a faint gold.

"Could be Trudie, or Andy. Did you ask them along?"

"I did. But it's not them," he replied. "I've got an observer ward by the front door. It's Arjun."

"Shit."

Arjun – Pranish's prickish older brother. Sorcerer extraordinaire. The show-off bastard froze an entire lake to show he could. Made sure to rub his power in Pranish's face anytime he could.

"Duer, hide," Pranish said. "Arjun isn't a fairy-fiend, but he's not averse to selling pixie parts."

Duer, probably already spooked by the events earlier today, flew up to the top of a tall shelf of books and disappeared over the top of some thick-bound tomes.

Pranish disappeared into the entrance hall, and arrived back with a tall clone of himself, wearing a similar style grey waistcoat. Arjun was the spitting image of Pranish, if not for a very warlock-like goatee.

"Your spark readings came back shoddy again, brother," Arjun hissed. "A wonder mom and dad keep sponsoring this place."

He stroked his finger on the side of a book shelf and grimaced at his finger. And I thought Pranish was a neat freak!

"Hello, Arjun," I said, no hint of warmth in my voice, but at least trying to act civil.

Arjun looked at me as if examining a yapping dog. He squinted, quizzically, and then recognition flickered across his features.

"Ah! The husk. Well, at least you keep appropriate company, brother."

Pranish whispered something under his breath but stopped as Arjun glared at him. Pranish clenched his fists and stared at the ground.

Oh, how I wanted to smack Arjun around a bit! But couldn't throw demanzite on my friend's brother. Wasn't good for relationship building. And couldn't punch him without the demanzite. I'd be a human popsicle before I could shout, "Down with the magi!"

Arjun strode into the room and snatched up one of the scrolls Pranish and I were crafting. He sneered.

"Wizardry." He literally spat out the word.

"The family business relies on wizardry, Arjun," Pranish said, too meekly for my liking, but I didn't know everything. Pranish had been broken down by Arjun. Was hard to build yourself up after that.

"Wizardry done by plebs. Done by husks like this." He indicated me. I stuck my nose up at him and looked as unfazed as I could. I wasn't really fazed at all. Magic was overrated. Preferred being a husk. I was more offended on behalf of my friend.

"So, what does that say about you?" a voice came from the doorway behind Arjun and Pranish. I glanced past them and saw Andy, leaning up against the wall.

"Excuse me?" Arjun said, shocked but maintaining his haughty, spark-reliant arrogance.

"Shard, and all magicorps, rely on husks to survive and thrive. So, what do you do? What does a sorcerer add to the workforce of a magicorp?"

"I'm powerful. Naturally powerful. I don't need any rivers of magic to grant me power. I control the elements."

He held out his hand and after a poof, an icicle appeared.

Andy whistled, derisively. "Ice blocks. Wow. What's the mark-up on those?"

"Andy..." Pranish said, his voice pleading. I didn't say anything. This was starting to get good.

"Who are you to chide me? A husk, or a sorcerer."

"A husk." Andy smirked. "A husk whose father is the Chairperson of the City Council."

Arjun's expression was slow to change from a sneer to shock, but when it did, his expression was very shocked indeed. He even backed away a bit. Excellent!

"Tell me…Arjun, is it? Is your subdivision of Shard up to date with its city paperwork? I wouldn't want my dad to, you know, make an example of your family business."

I swore that Arjun gulped! He looked at his brother, at me, and then left. Just as he was exiting, he shouted.

"Get those reports to me by tomorrow and we can forget about your spark results."

The door slammed shut.

"What a prick," Andy muttered.

"A prick with anger management issues," I added.

"And a lot of power," Pranish said. "That was risky."

Andy shrugged. "Sorry, not a fan of bullies."

Pranish's mouth twitched, as if he was about to smile, but he didn't. "Well, thanks. Anyway, didn't think you were going to arrive. You're even later than Kat! We're basically done."

Andy frowned. "That won't do! Any other enchantments I can help you with. I haven't done any wizardry but would like to get into it."

Pranish did grin then. Wizardry was his passion, after all.

"Well, if you two don't mind waiting for me, I can head to the store to get some vellum and wax. Always wanted to try making signet enchantments."

I waved Pranish off as he left, and then suddenly felt apprehensive. I was alone, again, with Andy. Well, not alone. Duer was still here. Why wasn't he coming out? Probably asleep. Duer slept a lot. So, it was just like last time.

"Howzit, Kat?" Andy asked, grinning. "Any cases? What happened with that Conrad guy?"

He took a seat opposite me. Directly opposite. It was a small table. I felt the warmth from his legs underneath the table and could see them through the glass-top. I looked up, inadvertently avoiding his eyes.

"Conrad is punishing me. Put me on some stupid case. Waste of time, so here instead."

"Why stupid?"

"Wants me to hunt a mimic."

Andy's lack of laughing revealed he didn't know what it was.

"A mimic is…"

"I know about mimics, but why is it stupid?"

"Well, we don't usually hunt mimics. No point. Easy to find. Easy to avoid. Even the cops can handle them. Oh, sorry…"

"Why sorry?"

"Well, insulting cops…"

"My dad is a Councillor, not me. In fact, I'm probably more anti the Council than you."

"That's hard to accomplish." I smiled, faintly. "I didn't know about your dad, though."

"Garce isn't a common surname. Henry Garce should have been a giveaway."

"I don't know the names of any Councillors. Well, that's a lie. I know about fuckwit Zieg DuToit, from sanitation."

Andy winced. "I hate that guy."

I laughed, relieved that Andy didn't like DuToit as well. Would have been pretty embarrassing if DuToit was his godfather or something.

Andy smiled as I laughed. And then, that dreaded and awkward silence.

"For the love of Brighid," Treth said, "Don't do this to me again."

But Andy broke it.

"About that date I asked about before…"

I froze.

"How does Friday sound? Day after tomorrow."

In my line of work, you need to make split-second decisions. You wait too long to decide if you're going for the neck or the ephemeral artery, and then you get bitten – or worse. There was no room for error or delay when on the hunt.

But I froze now. If Andy was a ghoul, I'd be dead.

"It's fine if you don't want to…" Andy raised his hands, as if to calm me.

"No, no," I finally said. "I want to go. Movie?"

Andy's grin shone pearly white. "We can see the new Manhunt movie."

"Can never say no to some good vigilante justice."

The inappropriateness of that statement only hit me a few minutes after I said it.

"Great! I'll book the tickets. Meet at the Waterfront Mall at 6:30?"

I nodded.

"Great, then it's a date."

Pranish stopped dead in his tracks, carrying four bags of stationary and enchanting supplies. My face was red as a devil's. Andy was grinning like a school boy.

Chapter 6.   Shopping

Trudie seemed more excited by the news of my date with Andy than me. She practically screeched with a girlish excitement usually unfounded in her calm and collected goth persona. She also insisted that we go shopping. The thought of it immediately filled me with horror, but Trudie was insistent. Before I could make the excuse that I couldn't afford to go shopping with my government fine over my head, I found myself draped with clothing that Trudie wantonly threw upon me as she looked for what she wanted me to wear. At least we were at the Riverstone Mall, the nearest shopping centre to my apartment, and not some exorbitantly expensive designer store in Old Town or the new weyline business districts.

I didn't know who was worse. Treth for forcing me to spend my hard-earned cash on tools for my part-time work, or Trudie who forced me to spend my hard-earned cash on tools for my love life. I blushed at that last thought. Didn't know why I even thought it. Wasn't my love life. It was just a date. Hanging out. Had done it with Andy before. Yet, there was always someone else there. This was different…

Far greater than my uneasiness at thinking of my impending date, was that overwhelming feeling that I do not belong in this kingdom of skirts and high heels. The colours were garish, the lights too bright, and the wait for Trudie to scour the multiverse for the perfect outfit…unending.

"We should be hunting," Treth whined. "When last did we slay an undead?"

"I know, I know." I sighed, heavily. "But Conrad's monitoring my MonsterSlayer account. If I get a job, he'll know. And he'll be pissed. I'm meant to be working the mimic case. Can't risk him cutting us loose. We get good work from him."

"When he gives us work…"

"Talking to yourself?" Trudie asked, peeking her head around the coat hangers. She was wearing blue mascara and black lipstick.

"Complaining."

Trudie stuck her tongue out.

"Come on! It's not that bad. You haven't gone clothes shopping in ages."

"Clothes shopped last week."

"Replacement jeans and vanilla t-shirts don't count."

"Still clothes."

"There's a big difference between your *clothes* and these…clothes."

She held up a white sleeveless sundress. An understated thing. Very unlike her usual fare. Not a hint of black. I grimaced. Not like my fare either. Zombie could grab onto it way too easily. And even a non-mutant zombie could probably claw and bite through the thin fabric. It was a death trap!

"Come on. Try it on before you make that face."

Before I could think up an excuse, or imitate my Britpop ringtone, I was forced into the changing room that seemed (at least to me) smaller than a ventilation shaft. A tiny (maybe not even tiny!) part of me would rather be surrounded by zombies.

"Beautiful!" Trudie said, shaking her head, self-satisfied. As if she was the one wearing the dress. "Andy will love it."

"Does it matter what I think?"

Trudie grinned. "Nope. Stay right there, I'm going to find some more stuff."

She disappeared again.

"Never seen her this excited," Treth said.

"Not sure what she likes more. Computers or clothes. Well, as long as I don't have to buy all this..."

"Kat?"

I spun on my heels at the voice and blushed a vivid red.

"Colin! What are you doing here?"

He pointed his thumb at the male changing room, next door to the female's. "Trying on a new suit."

I calmed myself, it was just Colin. Just my one-time attorney. Did it matter that he saw me in a dress that I'd be wearing in public anyway tomorrow?

"New suit? Does that mean new cases?" I asked, smiling cordially and hoping the red was disappearing from my cheeks.

Colin smiled. I noted his round-rimmed glasses. They made him look quite the nerd. And don't get me wrong, I mean that positively. Intelligence and *nerdy* interests are wonderful things.

"Yep. The prosecutor was impressed by my defence. Got me some clients."

"Congrats!"

"Thanks...well, how've you been?"

"I've been good. Just a bit bored. Agent got me on suspension. Well, not suspension. Running a case. Just..."

"Not a case you'd like?"

"Worse. I don't even think there's a monster to hunt."

Colin chuckled. "Usually, we celebrate when there isn't a real monster."

"Not me. I need to get paid. That fine isn't going to pay itself."

Colin laughed, and I couldn't help but smile back, and then Trudie reappeared.

She stopped and stared at Colin. Not stared. Glared. I contemplated at that moment, as I have often in the past, that Trudie was actually a sorceress, and that her affinity was for death stares. Colin flinched underneath the piercing gaze.

"Anyway, Kat, won't keep you anymore. Enjoy your day."

"You too, Colin."

He beat a hasty retreat.

"Who was that?" Trudie asked, venom dripping off her words. I must be threatening her plans. Rifts have mercy, her plans!

"My lawyer."

She didn't look like she believed me. Why? What was the big deal? I was just talking to a guy. Isn't that what she wanted? Did it matter which guy? Oh… no, I'm not interested in Colin. He's my lawyer. An acquaintance. Was just being polite.

"I think the dress you're wearing is the best," Trudie said, her scorn abating.

"So, we can leave?"

"This store? Yeah. The mall? No."

"Oh, Athena give me strength."

"You Greek now?"

"If it gets me out of here…"

A toothy grin returned to Trudie's face, white teeth surrounded by black lips. She was a bit sadistic.

We, and by that, I mean I, paid for the dress and we left the shop. I just hoped I'd get a job soon. The deadline on the fine wasn't strict, but I needed to eat.

En route to the next, my phone rang from my bag. No pockets in this damnable dress, so I almost missed the call. Got to it just in time though, as I swung my bag over my shoulder and dove my hand inside its contents.

"Hello?" I said, repressing that harried, anxious tone you so often get when answering a phone call you almost missed.

"Is this Kat Drummond?" came a familiar voice.

"Yep. Natalie?"

"Why are you not taking this seriously, Ms Drummond?" she said, no pleasantries. She sounded desperate. Tearful. I had the feeling it was taking all her strength to maintain any sort of composure.

"Excuse me?"

"My husband is gone. More people are disappearing, and that mimic is still out there. Do you think this is a game?"

I sighed. "Natalie, I don't think there is a mimic."

"Nonsense. Drake…"

"Drake scammed you all."

A pause. A long pause. I heard her breathing. I sighed again.

"You aren't one for letting people down easy, are you?" Treth said.

"I'm sorry about what happened to your husband, but there are no leads. No indication that a monster did it. I'm not a detective. I'm a monster hunter. If there aren't any tracks to follow, I can't do anything."

Another pause. I swore I heard sniffles. Oh shit. Way to go, Kat! Making a possible widow cry. Congratulations.

"There…there may be something…" Natalie said.

That surprised me. Any sort of lead in this leadless case could. "If anything could put me on the right path, then I can take this seriously, Natalie."

"Drake had a locker at the Kenilworth train station."

Kenilworth? That old neighbourhood? After the cataclysm, most of the well-to-do people moved out. No weyline. The train hadn't run in years. It was a desolate and abandoned suburb now. Only the horse racetrack still functioned.

"I don't have the key," she continued. "But with him gone, I don't think he'll mind you busting it open. There might be something there."

"It's something. I'll check it out. What number?"

"56."

"Thanks. I'll check it out."

I hung up.

"Who was that?" Trudie asked.

"Client."

Trudie winced. "Work tonight?"

I nodded.

"Don't be up too late. Remember? You have a date tomorrow."

I accidentally smiled. "I'll remember."

Chapter 7.   Locker

The night was dark, with hardly a star in the sky, and there were no streetlights to make it less so. The taxi service refused to drop me off further into Kenilworth and deposited me on the outskirts near the still relatively populated and prosperous Claremont. Kenilworth wasn't a slum, but still wasn't exactly safe. I felt as safe as I usually did on a job, though. Strapped with my twin dusacks, short Czech duelling sabres, my seax, and monster hunting armour, I felt as secure as I could in this city of magic and monsters.

I must admit, however, my audible footfalls on the wet, unlit street, were unnerving. At least I'd be able to hear if anything tried to sneak up on me. Well, most things. Treth would be watching for everything else.

I was following the old train tracks from Claremont. Run down, decayed. Like so much in this undead city. Portions of the tracks had been ripped up and sold for scrap, but many other parts of the old transport network remained. The theft was from the early days of the Cataclysm. People didn't know what was valuable any more. They just picked up everything they could. They hurt each other. They stole from each other. Or, so I heard. I wasn't alive back then. My parents were only kids then. It must have been a horrible time to be alive. Hope City wasn't so great right now, but it has to be better off than it was then. At least there was some semblance of order. Well, at least it was better outside of the slums. But walking through these unliving streets of dead Kenilworth, I couldn't help but feel that the death brought about by the Cataclysm had never really abated. We were living in the shadow of the Vortex, and that shadow brought an uneasy and inhuman darkness to the world.

"Sure is quiet," I said to Treth, glancing towards the empty train tracks on my right and blocks of dilapidated apartment blocks on my left.

"And wanting to fill up that silence?"

I rubbed the pommel of my dusack. "What gave you that impression?"

Treth gave a small chuckle. "This darkness and silence were normal on my world. I guess it would be normal anywhere outside the city. Probably even quieter. Even here, you can still hear this world's sounds of civilisation. Listen."

I stopped and did just that. And as Treth had said, I did hear civilisation. The distant hum of traffic, a siren in the distance, and the music of some evening concert. Hope City was alive, despite the darkness here. And that made my immediate surroundings seem even more dead. Black was only made blacker by the white surrounding it.

"Did you have cities on your world?" I asked.

"I did," Treth replied. "But not like this one. This is not a city. It is an unceasing jungle of stone."

"Earth once had a medieval period as well, with smaller cities."

"I have heard."

"Your cities must have resembled that of Dark Age London, or maybe the Renaissance Florence and Rome."

"In a way, perhaps. We did not have cars, or buses, or sirens, or everything else that contributes to this sheer cacophony of light and sound. But we did have magic. Magi oft built their spires floating above the ground, to avoid rabble and the monsters that infested the surface. Calidor was the largest city I ever…visited. It had tens of spires rising into the sky. Magnificent towers, hundreds of meters from the surface. Crafted of the finest metals, ivory, jewels and marble. They shone in the sunlight and glowed in the darkness. From all across the county, you could see at least the speck of their splendour. Hope City has nothing like that, but why would it? These towers on Earth rise higher from the ground than any floating spire, and a fraction of this city dwarfs the entire county of Calidor, if not the duchy. Gods, it dwarfs the Kingdom!"

Treth had some real anxiety in those last few sentences. He had become lost in his memory, and then shocked out of it. Nostalgia and trauma all tied into one. It was something I didn't envy. He used to have a home. A life. Another world. I'm not sure I'd have adjusted as well as he had if our roles had been reversed.

"Duer's tale was interesting, wasn't it?" I asked, changing the topic. I didn't want the silence to become absolute, despite the distant noise of the City. These streets were spooky enough as it was. Every window, dark. What people and beings could be staring out of them? What dark figure could be watching me? Waiting for me? It wasn't like the normal hunt. It wasn't a hunt. I wasn't expecting a zombie at the end of the trail, so if a zombie did jump out, that would make it genuinely frightening.

"It was," Treth replied, simply. He must have been self-conscious about his earlier outburst.

I frowned. Duer and Treth were otherworlders. Cosmic refugees. If given the choice, neither of them would be here. But they were. And they had both tried to make the best of it. It was something to admire in them. While so many Earthborn humans spent their lives doing nothing on their homeworld, tired of living and apathetic about everything, this pixie and knight made the most of their lot on a world infinitely far away from their homes.

A thought struck me, and I found new reason to keep my mind off the void black streets.

"Duer speaks good English. Can't read but speaks it well enough."

Treth hummed his assent.

"He must have learned it after coming through the rift," I said.

Treth didn't respond.

"But, you spoke English to me the first time we met. And you could read it…"

An uneasy silence fell. I'm not sure why. Did Treth think that I suspected him of foul play? That he wasn't who he said he was? That he was some Earthborn spirit, rather than an otherworldly entity? Well, now that you mention it…

"I have wondered about this myself."

I stopped on the street. There was a long drone as a car in the distance sped on its tarmac route.

"When I first came to meet you, I thought I spoke to you in my own tongue. But the words came out differently. Foreign. And when you spoke to me, I thought I didn't recognise the tongue, but I understood it. And when I finally came to see the script that I didn't recognise, I could read it."

"Do you think coming to Earth gave you the ability to speak Earth-languages?"

"I…I don't." Treth was contemplating. Thinking hard about this. I imagined him gripping his chin, even though I had no idea what he looked like. I sometimes imagined his appearance. The stereotypical gallant knight. Long, flowing blonde locks. A chiselled jaw. Some sort of *prince charming* Arthurian figure. I'd never thought to ask Treth what he actually looked like.

"When we've encountered other languages," Treth said. "I didn't understand them. I don't think you did either."

"Like?"

"Well, when people speak the language of the Zulu Empire, or…Afrikaans I think it is called…"

I winced. I never had a penchant for learning other languages. I was good at English, but Afrikaans and Zulu, not to mention many of the other languages common in Southern Africa, had always eluded me.

"I think," Treth continued. "That my comprehension of languages has something to do with my connection to you."

I raised my eyebrow. The clouds were uncovering the moon just about then, and the moonlight was reflecting white off the wet tarmac. I continued walking.

"So, you think I might be able to speak your language?" I asked.

I felt Treth nod. "I do. But not on purpose. When the time comes, I think you will be able to speak my tongue as well as I."

"Do you think it is just language we share?"

A pause. "No."

94

And that was that.

My sneakers crunched on the gravel of a long unused parking lot, situated next door to a facebrick tower, booms blocking the road and an old looking tin-roofed building next to the tracks. Kenilworth station.

"Why would anyone use the lockers in a ruin like this?" I asked out loud. I hoped there were no unsavoury humans (or beasts) around to hear me.

"A good place to hide. You don't need a fortress to guard your secrets if you keep them hidden well enough."

I nodded. Made sense. Drake, like any PI, would not want his info leaking into unpaying hands. Could always keep it in a safe in his house – but that's where rivals would first go to look. And better-known storage units weren't safe. Lockpicking spells were cheap to purchase and the wards against them were expensive. So, where better to hide your documents than in an abandoned train station?

"Well, here we go…"

"Why you drawing your sword?"

I didn't notice that I had. I was holding my dusack by my side. Moonlight reflected off the metal. I had been taking good care of it. No specks of rust. The twin swords had been serving me well. It was only fair I served them in kind.

"Peace of mind, I guess."

Treth nodded, sending the gesture as a sense of assent rather than a visual action. He agreed. He better. It was him who put me down this path. It was him that made me find peace in steel.

The gate to the train station platform was closed shut. Its iron bars and wire-mesh were brown with rust. Well, I imagined it was. Too damn dark to tell. I grabbed the bar of the gate with my free, gloved hand and shook. Metal rang out in the silence and I winced. If there were any fiends in the area, they'd be rushing to me right about now. At least I'd be ready for them.

"Not going to get in the civilised way," I said, more to myself than to Treth. I walked towards the tracks and to a lowered boom. A few rusty chains still hung underneath it. It was anyone's guess where the rest of the chains had ended up. I sheathed my sword and lifted myself over the boom, my feet crunching on gravel on the other side. An owl hooted, and I looked down the tracks into the blackness. No substantial light. Just the glint of moonlight on wet metal. The dark red, rainy sky did provide some silhouettes of two buildings with pitched roofs, both located on either side of the concrete platforms of Kenilworth station.

Crunch. Crunch. Crunch. I winced every time my feet fell on the gravel surrounding the train tracks, until I felt my way to the platform and lifted myself up. When I found my footing, I drew my sword again.

Time to see what I was doing. I put on my flash-light, attached to the strap of my bag. It let out an arc of milky white light that pooled out onto the grey concrete before me. Green grass and dandelions pushed out of cracks in the surface. At least there was some life here. But wasn't that always the way? Humanity gave way and other life replaced it. Neither good nor bad. Just life cycling into life. Well, that was how it was supposed to be. The way nature is meant to function. Nobody is meant to live forever, and something must always come after. And that was the problem with dark magic. It sought to circumvent the natural order. And it was my job to stop it.

"See anything suspicious?" I asked Treth. He was awfully quiet. Probably on high alert. I couldn't be the only one who found a long-abandoned train station creepy in the dark of a rainy night. It was odd. I could handle some zombies moaning but put me on a dark street and I start quaking. Perhaps, I'm a bit odd.

He shook his head. "Watching your back. Where would this investigator's locker be?"

"Hopefully dead-ahead. I don't feel like crossing the tracks to the other building."

"Dangerous?"

"No, an inconvenience. Trains haven't run in decades."

"Kat, what exactly is a train?"

I continued on to the building ahead of me.

"They're like buses," I said. "But longer. And they can only travel on these things called tracks."

"Ever used one? Are they better than these crummy buses we keep using?"

I shook my head. "Decades, Treth. I'm 19. Never seen a working train in my life. Only pictures."

I arrived at the door of a small building with a pitched roof of rusting metal. Peeled paint revealed brick. An old building. Pre-cataclysm. But its maintenance was newer. Someone must have been trying to do something with it in the last ten years. In Hope City's winds and rainy seasons, no paint should have survived this long.

The steel grate door was rusted open on its hinges. A faint breeze whistled through. Either an open door or window somewhere else in the building.

Well, here goes nothing.

I entered to the smell of dust, overgrown plant-life and burnt rubber. The floor was charred. Some drifters must have used this place to camp some time ago. Empty tin cans were also scattered across the floor. It wasn't a big building, which was lucky for me, as I was getting tired of this jaunt. I needed some sleep.

I found the lockers relatively quickly. They were small. About the size of a shoebox each and aligned in rows and columns across the entire back wall of the building. Many of their doors had been ripped off their hinges, their contents long gone. A few were still locked, but with dirty red exteriors. I scanned the rows. 54. 55. 56.

Drake's locker was easy to spot. It had the cleanest exterior. Dust and grime didn't settle as easily on something that got a lot of use. Drake, or someone, must have used this locker recently.

I removed my flashlight from my bag strap and put my backpack on the ground in front of me. I rifled through some assorted junk and found a scroll, tied up with one of my black ribbons. It was a scroll from Pranish. A lockpicking scroll the size of a sticky note. He looked mighty suspicious about my asking for it but didn't press. Good man.

"What did he tell me to do with this again?"

"Hold it on the surface and exert your will. Almost no weyline here, but there's enough power infused into that scroll for it to work."

I shrugged. Whatever that was supposed to mean.

I unwrapped the scroll. It was covered in what I could only tell was gibberish. But I trusted Pranish. It'd work.

I held it up against the locker and…

Didn't even have to consciously think about it. The scroll flared up into a golden flame that emitted no heat, and the locker door opened. Inside, papers. A lot of papers. And on top of them all: an envelope.

I opened it.

Chapter 8.   Voice of the Dead

I am dead.

I wasn't always. While writing this, I am very much alive. At least, I think so. At least, I've got a hunch I was alive. And in my line of work, you gotta start with hunches. But a hunch is just that. A hunch. And nobody cares about what your tummy's telling you. They want evidence. Proof and stuff. And that is where I come in.

Everybody's got a hunch about something. When your comfortable little world goes topsy-turvy, and things stop making sense, you get theories about why. You start suspecting stuff. But a suspicion is just that. Just the same as a hunch. Nothing. So, you start looking for evidence. Pieces of the puzzle to fill in the picture that is your hunch.

But not everyone's good at puzzles.

So, they hire Drake Callahan, private investigator. I'm good at puzzles. Well, at least I was. Real good at puzzles. And that's why I sought them out. Cause, at the end of the day, I just wanted to see the full picture.

People get different hunches, though. They think the picture at the end of the puzzle is something different. But only one of them can be right.

When a distressed little wifey came to see me, my hunch was her husband had run off with another woman (or a man). Common enough case. But, a hunch is just a hunch. And she had her own.

Monsters.

She said. Monsters had gotten her poor hubby.

I resisted laughing the entire meeting. Let her leave after collecting her details and then burst out laughing.

And then another wife came. And then a girlfriend. And then a boyfriend. A husband. A mother. A father.

Every client had the same hunch. Monsters. Monsters that the ticks at the Hope City PD refused to investigate. They must've had the same hunch as me. But, a hunch is just a hunch. And who am I to say that my hunch is better than all theirs?

So, I did my job.

I investigated the disappearances. I looked for monsters that I didn't believe existed. I almost didn't find any.

Almost.

I'm not a monster hunter. Hopefully, dear reader, you are. Cause, boy, we need one.

It took me a while to process what I saw in the labyrinth of brickwork at the Waterfront warehouses. I told myself I needed a break. That I was seeing things. That I must've been drunk. That I was overworked. Overtired.

But I wasn't. I was sober. Sober and energetic. And I saw a filing cabinet eat someone.

Yeah, sounds stupid. Funny, even. But ain't so funny when you see the blood. Ever seen a filing cabinet bleed? Red ooze from the cracks? White paperwork sticking out like tissues from an overflowing bin? Stained red...

I wish I hadn't.

Did my research on what I saw. Checked the bestiaries. Closest thing I could find was something called a mimic. A creature that disguises itself as inanimate objects to lure in prey and then gobble them up. I had actually learnt about them in pre-school. Told not to go opening treasure chests or the monsters'll get you. Thought it was just play-stories. I was wrong.

Mimics are real. And what we tell our kiddies is very important. But this isn't a treasure chest I saw. This was an honest to rifts, bland as they come, office filing cabinet.

And it had eaten a man, its drawer opening and closing, blood spraying as the man's legs and then feet disappeared.

Good gods of Olympus, it wasn't something I want to remember. But, it was something.

My hunch had been wrong. There were monsters. But, even if you know it's no longer just a hunch yourself, you gotta still have evidence to show everyone else. I'm no monster hunter, and we need one. But monster hunters need to know what they're up against. And they gotta believe there is something to hunt.

So, that's what I'm gonna do after writing this letter. This self-obituary. I'm going to go get the evidence I need. And then, I can be shot of this case.

But: if you're reading this – then I'm already shot of it. Just not the way I'd like.

So, dear reader, know that there's a mimic out there. It's got a taste for human flesh. It knows how to imitate what we trust. And it's probably digesting me right now.

All the best,

Drake Callahan, PI.

***

Drake's soundless voice in my head ceased as I folded up the letter and pocketed it.

"What do you think?" Treth asked.

"Either Drake went to a lot of trouble to plant this letter to cover his tracks, or there's a mimic that knows how to blend with modern Earth stuff."

"I don't think it's a lie."

I bit my bottom lip and considered the paper in my pocket.

"Neither do I." Which meant Drake was dead. I felt a tad guilty that I'd thought him a scammer. If his letter was telling the truth, he'd done his job. Went past the call of duty to do his job.

It was up to me to finish it.

"It's gonna be hard to track," Treth said. "Stationary. Camouflage. And despite the description of its messy eating habits, it seems it doesn't leave any trace of its victims."

"Doesn't matter," I said, securing my backpack and exiting the locker-building. "We'll find the thing. And we'll put it down."

Treth nodded.

"But before then," I couldn't help but grin. "I've got a date."

Chapter 9.   Dating

Andy was late. Or was I early?

I checked the time on my cell.

Shit, I was early.

"Told you," Treth said. I imagined an unbecoming mischievous and self-satisfied grin on the incorporeal knight's face.

"Shush," I whispered. Didn't want anyone hearing me talking to myself. Over the cacophony of mall-goers, I doubted anyone would.

I was standing by a gargantuan poster for the new Jet Gobbo movie, just off to the side of the entrance to the Waterfront cinema located in the bowels of Hope City's premier mall. I'd say I was standing in the shadow of the smartly dressed, pistol wielding super spy, but there were no real shadows to be standing in. Fluorescent lighting flooded the atrium with a white glow, preventing the formation of any sort of shadow or dark. While it was night outside, it may as well be midday indoors.

"This place is a lot busier than Riverstone," Treth said.

I nodded. "It's the foremost mall in the city. Riverstone is just for groceries. This is where everyone comes to play."

"What do they do here?"

I shrugged. "Hang out. Eat. Watch movies. Shop."

"But why here in particular?"

I didn't know how to answer. Instead, I checked the time again. I was very early indeed.

I had gotten home last night around 3AM, and then slept until midday when Trudie politely woke me up by flinging my duvet off me and then blaring AC/DC. Was all in all a pleasant way to be woken up. Trudie went on to lecture me about dating etiquette while I ate noodles for lunch, half-trancelike. Duer did not introduce himself. He thought Trudie was a witch.

I showered while Trudie prepared whatever it was that needed to be prepared. Wearing only a towel, I was leapt upon by my over excited friend, who adorned me with the white sun dress we had bought yesterday, makeup and a new red ribbon to tie up my hair in a ponytail.

"Splendid," Treth commented while I examined myself in the mirror, an extremely proud Trudie off to the side.

One could be forgiven for thinking she was a doting parent, aunt or older sister considering the way she acted.

Before me, stood someone I only vaguely recognised. The usual bags under my eyes had been expertly masked with all manner of cosmetic witchcraft. The rest of my skin was smooth and unblemished. My lips were tinted in a maroon hue. My hair, normally tied into a practical and messy bun, was draped in a ponytail across my shoulder, laying to rest on my breast. A red ribbon kept the hair together, at the base of the construct. Besides my new white, mid-thigh high dress, I was wearing stockings and black combat boots. The last one, a Trudie touch that I didn't mind. I'd much rather be wearing boots than high-heels.

"Perfection!" Trudie had said. I didn't know what to think. But I couldn't help but feel just a bit more confident, if a bit out of my depth. As odd a combination as any, but it was nice to feel pretty.

I soon shooed Trudie out of my apartment. After much pouting and excuses, she finally left. In the brief silence that followed, I could not help but focus on the intense quagmire growing in my stomach. Butterflies would be an understatement. It felt like a war. A battle between the excitement of this impending novelty and affirmation, and anxiety that things weren't going to work out.

In some ways, I would rather be preparing to go fight an undead abhorrent. I felt way less angst hunting prey than I did now preparing to meet Andy for a date.

A date. With Andy.

Oh, how life is a confusing bastard.

"You taking your swords, Kat?" Duer squeaked, when he finally made an appearance.

"Why would I?"

Duer shrugged. "To slay monsters?"

I chuckled at my usual answer for everything.

"I don't think I'll need them. Andy is likable enough."

Duer shrugged again, glanced towards Alex (who was napping on the couch) and then flew down to retrieve some honey from an open jar on the kitchen counter.

"Well, I should get going," I said, and made my way to the door. I put my hand on the knob and stopped.

My swords were on the countertop, next to my open backpack. Drake's last letter was inside the backpack, including his other dossiers that I had taken (just in case).

I wouldn't need them, would I? I was going a date. I was on my break. Not on a hunt! And it would be inappropriate to bring swords into a mall. Wasn't illegal. I had a card from Conrad to convince security to let them past checkpoints. But that wasn't the point. The point was I wouldn't need them.

But what if I did?

What if I had the swords at UCT last month…

Would fewer people have died?

Without any additional thought, I put my swords in my backpack and hoisted it onto my back. Trudie would have lamented that it clashed with my dress.

And, now here I am. Waiting outside a movie theatre for my first date in forever, my twin swords in my backpack by my side. Glancing at them, I hoped Andy didn't think me odd. Oh, Rifts, I shouldn't have brought them! He's going to think me a loony. Maddy Katty as Duer would call me.

A din rose above the usual chorus of chatter and footfalls on the tiled mall floor. I thought nothing of it.

"Kat, listen…" Treth said. His voice was different. Not the chiding he'd been doing for the past day, but back to his usual, serious businesslike tone.

I listened. Shouts. A scream. The music of trauma.

"I'm on break."

"Someone is in trouble."

I gritted my teeth and looked at the time. Ten minutes.

"Okay, I'll check it out."

I hoisted my bag onto my back and broke into a run towards the sound of the commotion.

Along the way, I overheard people speaking.

"What is it?"

"Someone's dead."

"Blood everywhere."

"Mob hit?"

"Monster?"

The last got my attention. A monster. My domain. And maybe a chance for a pay cheque.

I exited through some automatic doors. Security and police were blocking a crowd of onlookers from an alley between one of the restaurants surrounding the mall and a warehouse used as an indoor market. A cop wearing navy

112

blue was already putting up a police line. Typical. Will cordon off the area but won't give chase.

I shoved my way to the front of the crowd. Everyone was too enthralled by the novelty to mind. At the front, I saw blood. A lot of blood. Blood pooling out of a dismembered arm wearing an expensive watch.

"Please disperse," a cop shouted. Everyone ignored him.

I made my way to the cop and flashed the monster hunter ID I had received from Conrad.

"Monster hunter. What happened?"

The cop sneered. Civvie cops weren't so fond of monster hunters. Fair enough. We weren't so fond of them.

"Monster killed a man, miss."

He eyed me up and down, and then settled on the hilts of my swords. The dress must have confused him.

"What type of monster? Where did it go?"

The cop shrugged. Unhelpful tick!

"If you're wanting to stop any more deaths, tell me everything you know," I said loudly and firmly, channelling Conrad.

"It went down this alley. We didn't see it. Witnesses aren't helping."

Unknown monster. Shit. Well, can't be helped.

"Let me past."

The cop lifted the police tape and I went under it. I was careful to avoid the puddles of blood. A lot of blood. Messy eater, must be. Maybe, a lesser vampire? Nah. It's day time. Some sort of undead? A wight or gül could act independently of a necromancer. Could be a wraith, even.

This was worrying. I needed info. Didn't have any.

"Careful, Kat."

"I always am."

Treth snorted. He disagreed.

I drew my swords from my backpack and tightened the straps. Didn't like fighting with my bag on but didn't want to lose it by leaving it somewhere. I leant down to examine the arm. The bones were crushed. Not a clean cut. Was like it had been smashed with a warhammer. But there were some puncture marks. Nail sized. Small. Round.

"What type of beast has these teeth?" I asked out loud. I didn't care if the cops heard me. A lot of investigators spoke to themselves when on a case.

"Mutated undead can have all manner of teeth," Treth replied, but I heard in his voice that he wasn't certain this was from one of them.

I nodded, gloomily. I knew that all too well. It also meant I still didn't have a clue what I was up against. I scanned the puddle of blood around the arm. The puddle stopped after a few feet, but the blood didn't. A trickle continued as far as I could see. A trail. Something I could track. Excellent!

I stood from my crouch and followed the trail. I didn't hear anyone follow. Didn't expect them to. Hope City PD were cowards. Let a 19-year-old girl do the dirty work. They'd get paid their state salary all the same. Was a wonder they even showed up for work.

In the alley, the lights of the Waterfront were dimmed. Only a few yellow service lights flickered over their respective rusting doors. Concrete and face brick walls all around. Where was I? Didn't look like the Waterfront mall, with all its prestige, any more. Oh yeah. I had been here before. The warehouses. The place where the mimic victims had supposedly been eaten.

Mimic.

"Treth, think this is the mimic?"

"Could be. Fate has a sense of humour."

"Doesn't seem that funny to me."

Messy eater. Nobody saw what it was. And so, it should be. No monster could make it unnoticed into this area unless it was camouflaged properly. If Drake wasn't lying, this mimic could disguise itself as modern day stuff. People would notice a rift spewing out a demon, or an abhorrent skulking between the shoe stalls, but some crates with fragile stickers plastered all over them wouldn't attract any sort of attention. Except the attention of some curious bystander or dockworker, who'd soon be dinner for a beast.

The blood trail was thinning. I hoped it wouldn't dry up completely before I found the creature.

I noted, as I turned around a corner, my sword reflecting some of the light of an old, dusty bulb, that the butterflies in my tummy had abated. I only felt the healthy throb of my heartbeat, as the hunt was underway. I also noted that any thought of Andy was fleeting, as I examined the trickle of fresh blood and contemplated its cause. I was back on the job and while I felt fear, it was a healthy fear. The type of fear I was used to.

It felt good.

The blood trail was thinning drastically but before dispersing completely, stopped at the entrance to a warehouse. Its double doors were open. No light escaped. Just a void black.

"Why does it always have to be dark?"

"Because you never turn on the lights."

"Oh, yeah."

I entered the doors slowly, carefully, and reached out to the side of the door. Felt some metal and flipped a switch. With a roaring hum and an electrical crash, the warehouses fluorescent flood lights burst to life, coating the expanse with light.

It was a big warehouse. Too big. Too big seeing that there was no more blood to follow. Too many shelves with too many crates. A labyrinth. A labyrinth that may very well have a creature hiding in it. And not some bull-headed minotaur. This was a a creature expertly disguised as a part of it.

It was one of those times I was seriously considering why I did this job, but the lack of butterflies in my tummy was reason enough.

"Watch everywhere," I said, quietly before proceeding further into the warehouse.

"I'll do my best," Treth said, flatly.

I took off my bag and put it by the doorway. Opened it and withdrew a small scroll.

I held the scroll Pranish had made for me, closed my eyes and applied my will. I didn't feel any different, but I felt the scroll crackle and disappear. I should be coated in a thin layer of protective energy. Hopefully. Unfortunately, I'd only know when it would be too late.

I stood and walked into the labyrinth. No more blood to follow, so I went into the closest aisle. Kept my head swivelling like a searchlight. Treth would be watching every angle as well. Couldn't be jumped. Needed to be on higher alert than I'd ever been on before. Undead made noise. Even spirits made noise. A mimic was silent. Silent until it struck.

The shelves were lined with all manner of cardboard and wooden boxes. A big depot area. Lots of different brands on display. Everything from cardboard crates bearing Uhurutech logos to wooden boxes with the Shard branding. A lot of stuff. Probably valuable. Why was the door open, then? Was the security guard killed when either opening or closing the building? Would the mimic be smart enough to ambush a guard at the right time? From what I had read, a mimic only responded to being interacted with. It didn't seek out prey. It waited. So, was this not the mimic?

My gut told me it was the mimic…but that opened up more questions than it resolved.

My search through the labyrinth was slow. Quiet. My legs were cold as wind was entering through the open door and ventilation system. Definitely not the right clothes for the job.

The going was slow. I couldn't observe every package. I just had to hope I'd notice the mimic when I walked past it. That would probably be much harder than I thought. These things looked just like whatever object they were copying.

I also needed to get the jump on the mimic. Never wanted to be the victim of an ambush. That was a sure-fire way to end up dead. Always better to be the ambusher than the ambushed.

But how could I ambush something that looked like…I don't even know what it looked like. It could be anything.

Cardboard, wooden crate, the shelf itself, a cabinet, a chair...

I didn't know. But what I did know, was at this moment, my phone rang. And everything exploded.

"Kat!" Treth cried.

I dodged just in time as roars, slobber and fury pounced upon me.

It didn't look like any inanimate object. It looked like someone had painted a hairless Rottweiler to look like a wooden crate, and then sprayed water all over it. Oh, and it was the size of a van.

I rolled and landed in a crouch, a few meters from the beast. It swivelled and peered at me with six beady eyes appearing from its dark-wooden exterior. The previously solid looking wood was pulsating, like flesh. It was drooling between rows and rows of chaotically sorted nail teeth. A loud rumble emanated from its maw. I didn't see any limbs. Didn't mean it didn't have any. It could shapeshift at will. Could sucker punch me with an arm appearing out of nowhere.

A black tendril as thick as a lamppost shot out and skewered a cardboard box, letting cutlery fall onto the floor like blood and guts from a carcass. I had been standing in its way a second before. A second before it could have been me with a hole through my gut.

"Any ideas?" I shouted, side-stepping more from habit than a reaction to the mimic. Needed to stay moving. Never stop. Never be predictable.

"Keep small. Keep moving. Look for an opening."

I ducked as the mimic's arm-thing strafed above my head, clanging into the shelving units and sending stock tumbling.

"Right-o!"

I shot forward, swerving from side to side. Heat washed over me. Nauseating heat, emanating from flesh. I heard the gurgles and guttural vocalisations of digestion. How could I have missed this thing?

It spun on its blobby body and snapped forward, its jaw unhinging – if it even had hinges. I dropped to my knees and slid, slicing in an arc above me as I have done many times before. My blades slid off the mimic's deceptive skin. No cut. No blood. Shit.

"Rock hard skin," I said, rolling on my side under the mimic's elongated mouth.

"Must have an opening. Try the joints."

I let it shoot another tendril at me, dived under it and ran towards the opening where it had shot out of the mass. I stabbed at the base. My blade stopped. Was like trying to stab metal with metal.

Oomph. My head rang. Another tendril popped out and punched me square in the jaw. I had pulled back just in time, or else I'd have a broken jaw. Or worse. Perhaps, it should have been worse, and Pranish's spell had helped me. No way of knowing unless the spell ran out.

"I don't think we can handle this," I said.

I felt intense worry come from Treth. I seldom ever gave up. He was usually the prudent one. Must have worried him.

Hesitation. And then. "Watch for an opening, and then run."

I darted side to side, moving and waiting for another blow. I had no way of telling if the mimic was looking at me. Its six grey, glossy eyes didn't move. Didn't so much as blink. They might as well have been jewellery. Imitation eyes…

Fake eyes.

"It has real eyes hidden somewhere. Can you find them?"

A tendril shot out. I feinted left, it fell for it, and I ducked. We circled each other, this beast and I, looking for an opening. It wasn't the mindless organic trap that I thought it'd be. It was considering me, from its secret eyes.

"In its mouth."

"Excuse me?"

Crash... Two tendrils shot out simultaneously where I had just been standing, turning a pile of crates into splinters and a fog of packing foam. That was close.

"Its eyes are in its mouth. Above the tongue."

I looked closer, as well as I could at the beast while it was flailing its tendrils around. And as Treth had said, I saw a glossy orb at the top of its mouth, peering at me with a primal intensity.

How the hell am I supposed to blind it if it's in there?

I gulped. I knew how.

"I'm going in."

"What?!"

I surged forward, swords ahead of me, ready to deflect any oncoming blows. A tendril shot forward. I parried it away. The force of it almost snapped my wrist. Adrenaline let me keep going forward. I could complain about the pain later.

Another tendril. I dodged this one. The mimic jumped forward, its body sloshing and sounding like a dropped boulder all at once. Its mouth was only a few feet away. It widened its maw, ready to consume its rapidly approaching prey. I leapt, swords above my head, and launched myself off the mimic's lower lip, just in front of its sea of nails.

In seemingly slow motion, I flew through the expanse, sweltering fleshy heat rising towards me. It smelled like a thousand zombie hordes. Even I felt sick. And then a satisfying squelch. My sword landed in the beast's gum. It let out a rumbling squeal. Its eye, just in front of me, widened. With my free sword, I thrust forward. The eye popped and let out a spray of red goo. The mimic reeled. Its tendrils thrashed and battered me. I felt the bruises forming in real time. I couldn't dodge. Its flesh convulsed, and it shrank on top of me, its teeth drawing ever closer. I outstretched my legs as its mouth attempted to close and held its lips open as I did the splits. Should have continued gymnastics. This was not going to feel good in the morning.

"Let go, Kat!"

What? Let go? And let the thing eat me. I looked down at the black abyss underneath me. The thing was facing towards the roof, trying to let gravity drop me into its maw. Its teeth were coming ever closer.

"Drop. Just do it!"

I gulped. I let go of my sword and straightened my legs. I dropped as the mimic's teeth snapped closed above me.

Silence.

A low rumble.

And then the sound of shredding fleshy fabric as I cut myself out of the mimic from within. Gases hissed as they escaped the beast's body, and its rumble lasted for seconds before abating. The beast was dead.

But I was not alone in the beast's stomach. Before retrieving my sword from the mimic's mouth, I dragged out a comatose but very much alive man, covered in saliva and the blood of a very much dead man, missing an arm.

**

I left the man, uninjured, in the custody of the cops and paramedics. I had sent a photo of the mimic to Conrad. He'd handle the payment. I'd be able to pay off my fine and then some. The beast was dead now. Natalie should be pleased. Well, as pleased as one could be from justice. Didn't bring her husband back. Didn't bring Drake back.

But…that man had been alive.

Mimics didn't keep their prey alive. They ate them and digested them as soon as possible. But this mimic hadn't digested its feast, nor killed one of its prey. It had been keeping them. But for what? A mimic hunted to eat. It didn't preserve food. It wasn't intelligent. It ran on instinct.

But, so did dogs. And dogs could be trained.

"Kat…"

I was shaken out of my contemplation by Andy's voice. I immediately noticed my white dress, now covered in blood red and gut brown. I still had flakes of innards all over me. I had lost my ribbon and my hair was caked in saliva. I had been ignoring the stares from bystanders as I waited for the police to clean up the scene.

"Um, Andy…hey."

I looked for a way to escape. Couldn't find any.

"Some date…" he said.

"Yeah…sorry."

"Don't apologise. Work is work."

"Yeah."

I put my hands behind my back and rocked on the balls of my feet.

"Some work though."

Andy chuckled, and I managed to smile. Despite my embarrassment, disappointment, post-traumatic stress and tail-end of adrenaline, it was still a genuine smile.

Chapter 10.　Favour

Trudie took my standing up Andy much worse than he did. In fact, I hadn't seen her this angry with me since my first hunt, where I had almost had my head chewed off by a nightkin.

"Just one night! Couldn't you have just taken it easy for just one night?!"

"People were dying," I said, taking a bite of a chicken and mayo sub. It hit the spot.

"What if you died?!"

"We going to go through this again?"

Trudie looked at me with a piercing gaze. Her clenched fists shivered, and then calmed. She sighed.

"Just...yeah. Whatever."

She sat down with a huff.

We were sitting in the Gravekeeper Tavern. I had taken a day off to get myself healed of any injuries. The doc confirmed that Pranish's spell had worked. If it had not absorbed as much of the kinetic energy as it had, my face would look like a bowl of jelly. I said as much to him and he looked simultaneously radiant with pride, and sick to his stomach that I could have almost died.

Despite being comatose for most of her first time at the pub, Trudie had grown to like it. Still preferred the Eternity Lounge, for Athena knows what reason, but liked the food.

I went in for another bite as my friend pouted. I winced as some pain shot up my arm. I was wearing a brace on my right-hand. Had tried to chop that mimic a bit too hard and the shock to my wrist had damaged it. Wasn't anything too dire. Just needed to rely on my off-hand for a bit.

"Andy didn't seem to mind," I said, breaking the silence.

"Of course he minded!" Trudie burst out again. "He's just too polite to have said anything. He's a good guy. And you blew it."

I snorted. "I didn't blow it."

Or did I?

"Did he ask you on another date?"

I hesitated. "No…"

"You blew it!" Trudie said, half triumphantly. I don't think she knew what side she was on in this debate.

"Wasn't the place to ask me on another date. Was covered in blood and guts."

"What happened to the dress?"

I grimaced and Trudie noticed. "Don't tell me…"

I nodded, sadly.

"Shit, Kat…"

"There's a reason I don't go clothes shopping."

"It's not like you get eaten by a mimic every other day."

"Undead also make a mess."

The barkeep arrived and delivered Trudie her gin and tonic. She took a swig and turned back to me.

"Andy is a keeper, Kat. And the ball is now in your court. You need to catch him, or he'll get away when someone holds some tastier bait in front of him."

"That two or three metaphors?"

"Three, but that's beside the point. Are you interested in Andy?"

I didn't answer immediately. Instead, I stared into my half-eaten sandwich. I considered its texture, its dismembered meat and salad, the mayo so coyly dripping onto my hand.

"Aren't going to find the answer there," Treth chided.

I looked up. Trudie was swirling her drink in the glass, waiting.

"Yeah," I finally said. "I am."

"Then put some work in," she said, much calmer now. The tone was of a friend, not a nagging fishwife. "He probably thinks you'd prefer to be covered in guts than hanging out with him. That's not good for his self-esteem. I say: ask him out."

As has been the case in the past when I've wanted to end a conversation prematurely, Conrad arrived like magic. His grin was pearly white.

"My favourite monster hunter!"

"Hey, Conrad."

Trudie glared. Conrad ignored her. They'd never actually spoken, despite being around each other a few times. I should really try convincing Trudie that Conrad wasn't so bad. In fact, he's the reason I got a holiday. They should be the best of friends! Just ignore all the times he puts me in imminent harm, of course.

"Got a job for you."

I stood up, but he sat down.

"No need. Let's get a drink. I owe you one from the ghouls, don't I?"

I sat down again as Conrad signalled for the barkeep to bring two pints. I'm not sure of what.

"Anyway," he said. "Good work on the mimic case. Thought it was bogus myself. Was half hoping it was."

He shook his head, sadly. "Drake was a good PI. He'll be missed."

I nodded, plain-faced as I often was around Conrad. I was sad too, though. Drake had not been the scammer that I thought he was. Had been telling the truth the entire time. Died trying to prove himself.

"Things have cooled down now and solving that case has got you back in favour with the registry…"

"As if she needs the favour of the whatchamacallit…" Trudie interjected. Conrad ignored her, thankfully. I don't know what she was on about. Probably just looking for reasons to annoy Conrad (and me).

"That mimic case also proved that you could do some sleuthing…"

"Please," I interjected. "No more detective work. It was the right time and right place. I know how to stab things, not how to track something that doesn't leave tracks."

"You've done more than just stab, Kat."

The pints arrived, and he took a sip. It was lager. Condensation dripped down the translucent golden glass. I waited for him to speak.

"Got an exorcism case for you. A big one."

"It's always a big one."

Conrad waved the comment aside. "You ever heard of the Spectral Horseman?"

"Of Tokai manor?" Trudie asked, not a hint of mockery in her tone. She sounded genuinely intrigued.

Conrad, for the first time since I had known him, spoke to Trudie. "Yep. The Spectral Horseman of Tokai manor. You know about it?"

Trudie shrugged. "Used to live in Tokai. Was a common myth."

"Not a myth, or at least – not anymore. Tokai manor has a new owner, and the owner wants the spirit gone."

I paused and considered my almost completed sandwich and my unstarted beer.

"Could be interesting," Treth said.

"You've got details? The owner's, specifically."

"I took the liberty of arranging an appointment with them at the manor tomorrow. I hope you aren't busy."

I gritted my teeth. "I'll make a plan."

"Super!"

He took a long swig, and then departed before I had started mine. Trudie left soon after. Wanted to get some hours in on a new game or something. I half missed video games, but how could they compete with the real thing?

I finished my drink and sandwich and then stood up from the bar. The regulars were starting to file in and I didn't feel up to chatting with overly familiar and already drunk gentlemen.

"You forgot something," Treth said.

I didn't answer. Too many people. But I did look at where I had sat.

"Your suspicions about the mimic case," he continued. "Should ask Conrad about it. Ask to stay on the case, or to keep an ear out."

That was true. Something was off about that mimic. It wasn't like my research suggested. Wasn't like any mimic I'd heard about before. It was sophisticated. Smart, even. And it had not killed one of its victims.

I made my way to Conrad's office and reached for the door handle. Stopped, and then knocked.

I heard swearing, fumbling and some papers falling. Conrad opened the door, sweat matting his brow.

"Kat? What is it?"

"About the mimic…"

"Yeah, yeah. Sorry about putting you on the case. But you understand, right?"

"Not that…"

"It's just that got a rep with the registry and all that," he said, entering his office and letting me enter behind him. "Had to take you off the high-profile cases. Was practically forced to. Didn't want to."

He indicated the stacks of paperwork on his desk, chairs, shelves and floor. "It's not like I'm inundated with decent hunters."

"It's not that, Conrad. That's in the past."

He stopped and looked at me quizzically. I paused. Felt stupid for bringing this up. A bit insane, actually.

"I want to remain on the mimic case."

"What?" his single word and tone said a lot: why would you want to remain on a stupid, low-paying case that you have already completed.

"Hear me out."

He leant up against his deck. Some papers fell off and he clenched his fists but didn't bend down to pick them up.

"That mimic wasn't normal. Didn't have the usual mimic traits. Wasn't dumb. Wasn't disguised as a medieval artefact. And, its one victim was still alive."

Conrad shrugged. "Monsters adapt."

"Why just it, then? Why haven't we heard about this before? Why are mimic attacks so low if they have figured out how to successfully hunt humans? And: why keep the one victim alive?"

"I'm not a mimic expert, Kat. Neither are you. I'm sure there's some reasonable explanation."

"I think so too. I think someone trained it."

Conrad's one eyebrow seemed to almost rise in line with his greased back hair.

"Trained a mimic? Isn't that more unusual than a competent mimic?"

"We've got demonologists, necromancers and summoners. Even got druids who can control animals. What is so crazy about someone figuring out how to train and control a mimic?"

Conrad silently brought his hand up to his lip, contemplatively. Hopefully, he was genuinely considering it.

"Perhaps, Kat. Perhaps there is someone training a mimic."

I almost sighed in relief that he didn't think me crazy.

"Or perhaps you've ingested a little too much pixie dust. I saw your pixie friend when I picked you up for that one job."

I opened my mouth to retort.

"Go home, Kat. Got a real job tomorrow. Just forget about mimics and the big bad men telling them what to do."

I resisted going off in a huff and left the office.

"He may be right," Treth said.

"And he may be wrong."

"What's the plan?"

"Not much. No leads. No pay. I don't like the idea of people training mimics but can't go chasing hunches. Gotta pay the rent."

"Drake chased a hunch."

"And Drake's dead."

"Hmmm…"

I sighed, heavily. "No point dwelling on this. Got a real job. Exorcism. I hope you're not scared of ghosts after last time."

"I am a ghost."

"Really? Thought you were the delusional voice in my head."

"Hardy-har. Let's go home."

Chapter 11.   Ghost stories

When I usually run into pre-Cataclysmic ghost stories and myths, I tend to take them as poppycock. Can't blame me. Plenty of nuts reporting hauntings before spirits were even a real thing. Plenty of even nuttier people thinking they had magic spells and shit. Easy to dismiss them. Especially with all the info we have now disputing their crackpot theories. But when something from before the Vortex keeps happening after it, then I know something is up. Not something unexplainable. Magic and monsters are a science, now, after all. Can explain most things. And just because you can't, doesn't mean someone else can't either.

Take the Greek gods of myth and legend. Definitely pre-Cataclysm. So, were they just fun stories, or something else? We know now, cause of Athena existing in real life and all, that they weren't just myths. But how? No magic before the end of the 20th century, right? Well, not really. It seems there were some fantastical things before the Vortex. Rifts, like what we have now in earnest, sometimes opened up. Scholars call it *bleeding*. So, back in the day, other planes would *bleed* into our world. Difference was that back then, it was always intentional. Some magic user from another plane wanted to visit some weak mortal world, so they came to Earth for a quick vacation. While here, they sometimes interacted with humans. Well, not so much interacted as thoroughly screwed with.

Thus, myths were born. Sorcerers from other worlds were seen as gods. Monsters were spotted and informed urban myth for decades and centuries, despite said monster promptly dying as it failed to find its staple food source of lumpel berries (poor Bigfoot).

Post-cataclysm, these myths started to make more sense. We had things to test with, after all. And it helped that plenty of the immortals that had screwed with us humans in the past had been brought onto Earth and trapped with us. They had a lot of explaining to do. Luckily, no one bore a grudge. Hard to stay angry with Zeus for stuff he did to your two-thousand plus old ancestor.

But not all myths are so explainable. Plenty of cults from the 20th century, especially those dealing with the so-called supernatural and paranormal, were soon thrust into obscurity. Ghosts are only profitable to scam artists when the ghosts don't exist, after all. But, as I said, not all these stories died so easily after the Cataclysm.

The spectral horseman is one of those pre-Cataclysmic myths that, like any stubborn post-Cataclysmic undead, refused to die. In fact, after the Vortex appeared, it became even harder to kill off. Kind of hard to dismiss a ghost story when said ghost is looming over you on its equally ghostly horse.

Before going to the manor to visit the new owner, I invoked my major in history and went to the archives to read up about the ghost of Tokai manor. What I found was a chilling narrative, neglected by time but sturdy enough that not even the forgetfulness of the human consciousness could bury it forever.

***

It was a scorcher. More so than any usual summer day. Frederick Eksteen hoped it wouldn't put a damper on the New Year's Eve festivities. Well, it wouldn't if his father, Petrus, could help it. Put enough booze down someone's gullet and they'd sing and dance through hell's inferno. And Frederick's father had more than enough booze. A cellar full. And no matter how much liquor was drunk, the cellar was always filled up the next day. Some people thought it was magic. Frederick knew better. Every time

141

the cellar was restocked, the coffers became just a bit lighter.

But it couldn't be helped. Petrus loved parties. Loved socialising. Loved to make people laugh at bad jokes that they couldn't remember nor hear over the music, the cacophony of voices and miasma of liquor. Petrus, Frederick's father, loved the party more than anything else.

Frederick sighed while grooming his chestnut mare. He had ridden her to Groot Constantia nearby in the heat of the day to pick up some more bottles of wine for tonight's party. It wasn't fair on her, but Frederick's father was insistent. Frederick stopped and frowned. Wasn't fair on him either. It wasn't his party. Wasn't his job or anything. It was a favour to his father to fuel his insatiable hobby. Wasn't worth getting riled up over, though. Petrus, Fred's father, was a good man, at his core. He just wanted to make people happy. And, it was New Year's Eve. If there was any reasonable excuse to party, this was it.

"Fred!" Petrus called, coming towards the stables bearing a pair of wine glasses.

Frederick smiled, even though he didn't feel like it, and turned towards his father. He noticed that the glasses were engraved with finery. Their rims were gold.

"Look at what I got for the party, Fred!"

"I sincerely hope they are a loan, pa."

Petrus faked a frown and then laughed, as if what Fred had said was the funniest of jokes.

"Of course not! They are an investment. People can tell the difference between a loan and a true asset."

"And do they care?"

"Of course! It is all about respect, my boy. All about respect. And we mustn't let the other estates bring in more respect than us."

"Why?" Frederick asked honestly and straightforwardly.

Petrus pondered the question and then slapped Frederick hard on the back jovially.

"For the sake of it," he said with a laugh. "So, I host these parties. You will thank me some day. This estate shall make it into the history books. All the colony shall envy you and your family. And talking about that…"

Frederick's cheeks reddened. Petrus grinned in response. A childlike, exuberant grin. Frederick often wondered if Petrus really was his father, or just some greying older brother.

"Anne tells me that Catherine will be at the party tonight."

Frederick didn't think that his cheeks could get any hotter. They did.

Petrus laughed again, and patted Frederick on the back again, but much lighter.

"This is going to be a night to remember, my boy. The most memorable party we'll ever have."

Frederick didn't respond. He only turned back and continued caring for his horse.

Guests started arriving at sunset, which was late this time of year. Dinner was, suitably, to be served late. Even the nights were hot this time of year, but the Cape Dutch architecture of Tokai manor maintained a comfortable coolness through thick stone walls and high ceilings. Chilled wine also kept people at a reasonable temperature, until they were too drunk to care. Dinner was lavish, as it always was. Frederick wasn't sure where the money came from, but his father always managed to find enough to table the most massive banquets. Only the best for his guests, after all.

After dinner, the dancing, renewed drinking and small-talk of the inanest nature began. Frederick stood to the side, as he always did, watching. Petrus was regaling his socialite buddies with gossip from other parties and the neighbouring estates. And Catherine was standing alone on the other side of the dance floor, an almost empty glass of red wine in her hands. Frederick was glad for the flush that liquor brought on, as it camouflaged his much more unbecoming blush.

"Off to the side as usual, eh?" Frederick's friend, Piet, said, leaning against the wall. He looked to where Frederick had been staring and made an oh expression.

"The lady's daughter? High stations you doth desire indeed."

He grinned.

Frederick took a sip of red and didn't reply.

"Come on, Fred. Go talk to her. The night is young yet, but it is slowly wiling away. Make the most of it. Will be a good start to the new year."

Frederick grumbled some excuse that neither convinced Piet nor himself.

"I'm your friend, Fred. And as a friend, I know what is best for you. Either, go talk to her now, or I'm calling her over here."

"No!" Frederick said just a bit too loudly. Some partiers stopped to stare. Frederick slumped his shoulders and a bit quieter, repeated. "No. I'll go talk to her."

Piet grinned. "That's the spirit. I'm rooting for you."

For as much as that was worth, Frederick thought, but he crossed the dance floor all the same. Halfway across the room, Catherine looked up and smiled. Frederick couldn't help but smile back, despite the lump in his throat.

An eternity later, Frederick arrived in front of Catherine. Froze. And then as Catherine was about to speak, bowed low, spilling some wine onto the floor.

"Would the lady like to dance?"

A pause. A dreadfully, murderously long pause.

"I would, if it pleases the gentleman."

Frederick looked up and Catherine was smiling. That beautiful, enchanting smile. Frederick felt that he could die right now and if that was the last thing he saw, he would die happy.

Frederick extended his arm and Catherine accepted. She was warm. But it wasn't an unpleasant warmth in this heat. It could never be, if it was Catherine.

They made their way to the centre of the dance floor and, once again, Frederick's heart leapt into his throat.

What type of dance? Everyone around them were doing something different. Slow dances, exuberant jigs, folk dances.

Frederick froze up, but Catherine smiled. "Let's do something slow. It's almost the new year. I want to conserve my energy, lest I swoon."

Frederick nodded and began a slow waltz. Despite Frederick's shyness and introverted nature (at least compared to his father's socialite ways), he had received tutelage in dancing, and fell into the dance smoothly. Catherine closed her eyes and let the soundless melody and motion of the dance carry her away. Time melted, and Frederick lost track of everything around him. All that mattered was the girl before him, and the dance.

Catherine, leaning in, broke him from his reverie. She opened her brown eyes.

"Thank you, Fred. I'm glad you asked me to dance. It's the first time."

Frederick shrugged. "A good way to end the year and start the next."

Catherine laughed. It was beautiful. "Well, I hope it isn't a last time…"

"Fred!" Petrus called. "Fred!"

Catherine let go of Fred, much to his sorrow, and made way for Petrus to enter the fray.

Even with his own semi-intoxication, Frederick could smell the waves of drunkenness rolling off his father, who staggered side to side to add to the effect.

"Fred," he repeated. To his side was his brother, Jacob, who looked equally drunk. "My boy, your uncle said the darndest thing to me. Said… you tell him, Jacob."

"I said," Jacob said with fewer slurs, despite his reddened cheeks and red-stained teeth. "That despite your admirable skills in horsemanship, you could not and would not attempt to ride your horse into the house itself, so to amuse the guests and make the ladies swoon."

"Dear uncle," Frederick replied. "You are right in your assessment. It is much too dangerous. The veranda that makes this wondrous house so iconic is much too high."

"But you ride your horse on the mountain all the time," my father said. "Are you suggesting that the steps leading up to my house are much higher than the steps leading up Table Mountain? For I do not doubt that, considering the glory of this house."

Jacob, Catherine and a few bystanders laughed at the jest. Petrus grinned. His teeth were also stained by the red wine.

"Yours is a good mare, my boy. She'll do well in this. Humour your father, especially as he has money riding on this."

Frederick couldn't help but roll his eyes. As well as being an addicted socialite and borderline alcoholic, his father was also a compulsive gambler.

"I have a full pound sterling on you being unable to rouse your mare to even mount the steps," Jacob added.

Frederick shook his head. "It is much too dangerous."

"Come on, Fred," one of Petrus' friends piped up. "I'll add a pound to the wager."

"I've seen you ride. You can do it. Count me in," another added.

Frederick gritted his teeth and looked at Catherine. Her smile had not dimmed. His eyes must have been asking for her opinion, as she said.

"Do it quickly, Fred. I'd like to wish in the new year with you."

That was assent enough.

"Hand me a bottle!" Frederick said, to the cheers of everyone around him. He chugged the red in a single breath and after that liquid courage, left the building to the night summer's warmth. His mare neighed as he entered the stable. She must have smelled the liquor on his breath, as his attempts to calm her took a while.

"It's okay, girl. It's okay. We're going for a ride."

Eventually, she calmed. Frederick looked at the saddle nearby and his riding equipment. In this dark and his drunken state, he didn't think he could negotiate the equipment onto himself or the tack onto the horse. He shrugged, to nobody in particular. It would be a short ride. He had ridden his mare bareback before. He could do it now for this short trick. He managed to get the bridle bit onto the mare and negotiate the reins into what looked like the appropriate position in the fogginess of inebriation. It'd be enough, he thought.

Frederick was a good rider, even in his state, and his mare was well trained. She made her way out of the stables and up the lawn towards the manor. Lamp and candlelight from within made the high-rise manor look like a mystical castle. Its steps looked a thousand miles high from the bottom.

Frederick gulped.

"Come on, lad, let's see how you ride," someone called from atop the veranda.

"Well, girl," Frederick said. "Here we go."

First, the mare thought the prospect of the steps ludicrous. She balked, but with coaxing, she mounted them. Frederick held on for dear life as the incline grew, and the mare climbed the steps with increasing speed. With every step, he felt he was falling further and further back.

That last drink was a bad idea...

And then he was on top of the steps, with people cheering around him.

"That's my boy," Petrus cheered, a bottle in his hand.

"Not yet," Jacob said. "The wager was that he'd take the beast through the house. Greet the rest of the guests."

"Well, let us go," Frederick slurred.

The mare was incredulous at Frederick's directions but followed through. They entered the wide hall of the manor. The hooves were heavy on the hard-wood floors and made creaking noises over the revelry in the next room.

Frederick and the mare entered the party to playful screeches, cheers and a toast to Frederick's horsemanship. Frederick beamed as a man only could when he had proven himself through some odd feat. People came to stroke and fiddle with his mare and while sober, he would have stopped them, in his state he could only look for Catherine, to ensure that she had seen what he had done. But she was nowhere to be seen.

"Anybody seen Catherine?" Frederick asked, quite inappropriately. None of the revellers paid him any mind. They were too busy drinking, chatting, exchanging bets with those who had won and lost the wager.

The mare was anxious, twitching and swaying. Frederick eventually noticed and placed his hand on the mare to calm it. It didn't like the noise. Didn't like the fumes. Didn't like the behaviour of these humans acting more animal-like than animals.

A man was trying to coax the mare to drink from a brandy glass. One of Frederick's father's new gaudy goblets. The horse was recoiling from the drink, but that man was insisting, grabbing the horse by the mouth.

Frederick, anxiety rising at the absence of Catherine and the stress of his horse, looked around. He was boxed in by partiers.

"Make room!" Frederick shouted. Nobody listened.

The man wouldn't stop trying to make the horse drink. He was being egged on by his comrades. The horse was getting really spooked now, looking for space that wasn't there.

Frederick couldn't blame her. The adrenaline he had developed and turned into triumph during his feat was coagulating and turning to angst. To extreme anxiety. And where was Catherine?

And eventually, the horse could no longer handle it. It rose up on its hindlegs and neighed. Luckily, everyone in the way of the hooves recoiled. Some laughed.

"Oh, Petrus, your son may not be able to control the beast after all."

"Nonsense! He is controlling the mare perfectly well. Aren't you, boy?"

Frederick, holding tightly and desperately onto the reins of the horse, didn't reply. He was losing control. And where was Catherine? Where was she to see his triumph?

Wide-eyed and anxiously, Frederick scanned the room. Catherine still wasn't there. And neither was Piet.

Piet. Frederick's friend.

His friend.

Before Frederick could ponder the terrible thought for any longer, the mare finally had enough. She exited the room at breakneck speed. The people who screamed and laughed were equal.

For Frederick, time slowed. For the mare, all that mattered was exiting this dreadful place, embracing the cooling night air and getting back to the stables.

The door was open, and the veranda was ahead. The veranda with its twin steep staircases.

Frederick only needed to slow the horse down. A slow walk down the steps would be safe enough. It was summer. No rain to wet the steps. No chance of slipping.

But the horse wasn't slowing down, and as Frederick pulled at its reins, it only balked and ignored him. Instead, it charged to the centre of the door. Right towards the half-wall separating veranda and a long drop.

I can stop her, Frederick thought. But he couldn't. And in its bestial frenzy of fear, the horse leapt over the half-wall. Frederick closed his eyes. He smelled liquor. He smelled horse. And he smelled Catherine's scent, clinging to him.

He was drunk, and the tornado of inebriation still made the world swirl. Wind rushed up against him. And he breathed, one final time, and said.

"Catherine."

Chapter 12.   Dancing

Tokai manor was an historical monument long before the Cataclysm and remained so. That meant it was protected territory. For all that was worth under a government that couldn't keep zombies out of half the city. Luckily, private owners had saved it and kept it relatively well maintained throughout the decades.

It was a unique structure and I couldn't help but become a bit excited gazing at it. It was historically significant. Not for any grand historical event, or even for who lived in it before. It had normal, if rich, owners and had not been linked to any wars, political conspiracies or drastic criminal holdouts.

The only event linked to it was the story I have just told, and the haunting that will be explained in time.

But it is not this story that made Tokai manner important. It was its architecture. Tokai manor was an atypical Cape Dutch building, probably thanks to its very unDutch-like French architect. While it had some of the essential architectural quirks of Cape Dutch architecture, it was ultimately made unique by an elevated veranda, called a *stoep*, flanked by two curved flights of stairs. Round pillars kept up a roof over the veranda, with a pitched thatched roof covering the rest of the building.

A thin, elderly lady wearing a black trench coat and matching dress pants stood at the base of the manor to greet me as my taxi drove up and dropped me off.

"Ms Drummond?" she asked. She had short, spikey white hair. Her lips were blood-red. I'd have thought her a vampire if I wasn't educated enough to know how real vampires looked.

I put out my hand and she accepted it.

"I am Miriam LeBlanc. Owner."

I recognised that name. But where…

I almost gasped. Fortunately, I held onto a bit of my dignity and restrained my outburst to a slightly excited question.

"The vampire expert?"

Miriam laughed, goodnaturedly. "Expert is relative. I do dabble."

"Dabble? You practically wrote the textbook on vampirism. I've got you to thank for all the ghouls I've slain."

"I'm glad my studies have served you well." I could not help but notice a hidden glower behind Miriam's smile. Was I inappropriate?

"Please, Ms Drummond," she said, indicating to follow her. "Let's have some tea while I speak about something very much out of my area of expertise."

"Spirits?"

Miriam did frown properly then. It was a grimace that looked quite natural on her. "Exactly."

We made our way up the stairs that Frederick had scaled with his mare two centuries prior and entered the house. It was a very peculiar experience, walking down these preserved halls that I had only recently read about in such vivid detail. Was like living a dream.

Miriam led me into a room not mentioned in the story. Despite the well maintained historical façade, the kitchen was modern and equipped with a fridge, shiny countertops and appliances.

She indicated for me to sit and then put a kettle on a gas hob. One of those whistle stovetop kinds. Old fashioned, to contrast with the modern sleek steel gas stove.

"I bought the manor about a month back," Miriam said, taking a seat herself. "I'm not from Hope City, as you probably know."

I did. Miriam hailed from Verdun, a city state in France. I didn't pick up any French accent, however.

"I am a fan of your work, Ms LeBlanc. It is miss, right? I am not too clued up about the person behind the pages."

Miriam nodded. "It is miss. My work takes me around the world and I could never find anyone willing to put up with my habits. But I digress. I bought this manor on a whim, as my work brought me to Hope City. I wish to study some rift-borne sites on Robben Island."

"A new book, I hope."

I truly did enjoy LeBlanc's work. I had been introduced to her crisp and no-nonsense writing in first year Undead Studies. It was a rare thing to behold – an academic that could get to the point. But, Miriam wouldn't call herself an academic. Or an expert, it seems. She was just a woman with a passion, and that passion had led her to become one of the leading specialists in vampirism.

Miriam smiled, faintly. This hint of satisfaction looked uncomfortable on her. She seemed to prefer frowning to smiling. The kettle was rumbling as it heated its charge.

"Hopefully. If I can find enough source material."

"Can you give me some spoilers?" I gave her my most pleasant and endearing smile. She laughed.

"In time, yes. But this isn't the occasion to discuss vampires and coming from me that means something. I reached out to Conrad, despite my better judgement, because I needed someone who understands the ethereal. He recommended you highly. And not his insincere car salesman praise. I think he really believes in you. That means a lot."

So, she knew Conrad. Interesting. Also, interesting that he thought highly of me. Would be nice if that had translated into him not benching me earlier.

"I read through the dossier," I said. "Did the research. I'm not a professional exorcist by any means, but I've dealt with spirits before."

"As Conrad said. You've dealt with lesser vampires and, while spirits are a different matter, the fact that you're unscathed after so many vampires shows that you've got grit."

"Thanks."

"Not a compliment. An observation."

"That makes it better."

The kettle started to whistle, and Miriam stood to prepare the tea. "How do you like it?"

"No milk. No sugar. Rooibos, if you have it."

"Health-nut or nihilist?" she asked.

"A bit of both."

Miriam deposited the teabag into a mug and poured in the water. The translucent boiling liquid started to go a rich reddish brown as it mingled with the tea leaves. Miriam prepared my tea, brought it to me and then made her own – rooibos with two sugars and milk. Still on the darker side, though. Wasn't like Pranish took his tea. He took it mostly milk. Was basically just milk.

Miriam finally sat down herself. Both our mugs were on the table top, awaiting the correct temperature for consumption.

"As the dossier says," Miriam said. "The spectral horseman appears seemingly at random on the grounds.

160

He takes the form of a glowing human figure atop a horse, wearing period clothing. I cannot understand his speech, but it resonates and pierces the mind as I hear spiritual language often does. On nights when he appears, I cannot sleep. His ethereal glow stabs through even the blackest curtains and his presence brings angst and torment."

She was a lot wordier in person...

"I wish to sleep, Ms Drummond," Miriam said with palpable resignation. "And with a social evening I have planned at the end of this week, I require a spirit-free estate to entertain my guests. While I think many of them would be amused by the novelty of a ghost, I'd rather have the spirit off my property."

The tea had cooled down and I took a long sip while figuring out my response. I placed the mug down and leaned forward.

"Spirits are complicated, Ms LeBlanc. Especially ghosts. Unlike other ethereals, they can't just be exorcised with purity seals, holy salt and purification chants. They require delicacy, and knowledge of the ghost in question."

"And? Do you think you can handle such a *delicate* matter?"

Was that sass? I did notice bags under LeBlanc's eyes, hidden under makeup. She must really be tired. Tired and testy.

"I have looked into the legend of the ghost that haunts this place and I believe I have enough knowledge to exorcise it. But as I said: it is complicated. Ghosts are remains of the dead's semi-consciousness. To exorcise them, you need to bring the spirit to the place of their death and then aid them in passing. This can be either through persuasion or force. I can do both in tandem to make sure."

Miriam frowned. A different type of frown than earlier. The type of frown you give when you are used to understanding something but currently can't make head or tail of it.

"What will you need from me?"

"Frederick Eksteen, the man I believe is the ghost, died on New Year's Eve some time in the first half of the 19th century. He was an avid horseman. So much so, in fact, that he died with his horse after a fatal accident during the party. He died on your front lawn. So, I need to get him there, so I can give him his final rites."

"All sightings of the ghost have been in the forests and avenues near the estate. Never on it."

"That is to be expected. Ghosts seldom relive their final moments. And like any creature, they have an instinctive sense of self-preservation. They have to be coaxed into returning to their place of death, so to risk exorcism."

Miriam sighed. "And I thought vampires were complex."

I smiled, faintly. "My specialty is non-vampiric undead, so you can try to understand how I felt trying to get into this. But despite the complexity: I have a plan. You said you were having a party this weekend?"

Miriam nodded.

"Frederick died during a party. A party of a similar nature may coax him towards the manor."

"What type of party?" Miriam raised her eyebrow quizzically.

"Nothing too intense. Ghosts are vague creatures. The general feel for an event can attract it. As long as the general activities of the party are the same, I trust that Frederick will make an appearance."

Miriam sighed. "I was hoping to be shot of him before the party, but it sounds like it can't be helped. What should I ensure happens?"

I took another gulp of tea and pondered. "Alcohol and its consumption, and dancing. Those were the two things that stood out in the story."

Miriam nodded. "Liquor was already to be provided, thanks to this borderline magical wine cellar, and dancing can be arranged. Anything else?"

I shook my head. "That should be enough, Ms LeBlanc."

I polished off my tea and we both stood.

"What time should I arrive for the party?" I asked.

"7pm. I hope that the earlier darkness won't put off the ghost."

"It will be fine," I said, and shook her hand. "I look forward to the party and eliminating your ghost troubles."

"As do I, Ms Drummond," she said, leading me outside towards a waiting taxi.

As I entered, she stopped me.

"Feel free to bring a plus one. It may be work, but it is still a party."

I smiled, despite the anxiety that statement sent roiling through my body.

***

A plus one?

A plus one.

A plus one!

"What's the big deal?" Treth asked. "Just bring Andy. Can make up for last time."

If I could have looked pointedly at Treth, I would. He must have felt that desire, as it silenced him.

I had arrived home, pondering the exorcism case without giving any thought to Miriam's last words – until I closed my apartment's front door behind me. Then my cheeks flushed, and I stopped moving.

"What is it, Kat?" Duer squeaked, swooping down. Even Alex must have sensed something, as he ignored the pixie and sat in front of me, swishing his tail.

I bit my lip. It wasn't a big deal. Why was I acting like this? Was just a job. Didn't even have to bring a plus one. Could just come alone. Professional-like. Just business.

But I felt that wasn't the right decision.

I owed another date to Andy. And if Trudie somehow found out with her near omniscience that I'd passed up a perfect opportunity to make it up to Andy, she'd probably murder me with the corpse of a unicorn she'd just murdered herself. But was this a perfect opportunity? I'd be spending the party shouting at a ghost and throwing salt at it. Wasn't exactly romantic.

But I could tell Andy what was up. Clear disclaimer. He'd come in knowing full well what the party would entail. And, he'd see me in action.

That last thought brought an involuntary smile to my face. I caught myself feeling premature pride, and realised I was still standing by the front door.

"Kat?" Duer asked.

I felt Treth inquiring as well, staring intently from his incorporeal chamber. Why were they staring? Oh yeah, still standing…

I walked forward, one step at a time. Satisfied, Alex wound his way around my legs. Duer followed. I made my way to the couch and slumped down. Pondered some more, and then with a snap of finality, withdrew my cell phone.

"You're actually going to do it?" Treth asked, aghast.

"Sssshhh," I said, listening to the dialling tone.

"I didn't say anything," Duer said. I waved at him to be silent.

"Hello?" Andy answered.

"Hey, Andy. It's Kat."

"Hey, howzit?"

"Good, good…" I said.

A pause. Oh, Vortex, a pause!

"So…" Andy said. I interrupted him before the pause could re-emerge.

"I've got a job coming up, this Saturday. Involves me exorcising a ghost. Thing is, it is a party. Need the party to lure the spirit out and all. Drinking, dancing and stuff. Need it to be as convincing as possible for the ghost to be lured in…"

"Needing all of us to come get drunk to exorcise a spirit?"

"Not all. Just…just you. Got space for a plus one."

"Oh…"

"It's fine if you're busy! Not a big deal. I'm sure there'll be enough people to coax the spirit…"

167

"I'd love to come!"

My breath caught in my throat. Why? Why was I acting like this? Was it that I really liked Andy?

"Great!" I finally managed to say. "I'll text the details."

"Awesome. I'm looking forward to dancing with you."

We hung up.

Dancing…

With Andy.

Actually, scratch that…dancing at all.

I never danced. Well, one could think of my fighting style as a dance of sorts. Sure, I even melodramatically called it a dance of death before. But I'm pretty sure there's a big difference between the waltz and swishing a sword around.

"I…" Treth said, hesitation. "Can teach you to dance."

"What?" I said, genuinely shocked. Duer cocked his head. Still wouldn't believe my explanations about Treth.

"I can teach you to dance," he repeated, with a little more confidence.

"What do you know about dancing?"

"No dance a human could do," Duer answered.

168

"Not you," I said, shushing him. He shrugged and flew off to do whatever pixies do. Probably snorting vodka and honey while growing mushrooms where he thought I couldn't find them.

"I used to dance. When I had a body, I mean."

I raised my eyebrow and sat forward, hands clasped in front of my face.

"Really?"

"Hey, do you need help or not?"

Sore point?

"Okay, Treth. I'll bite."

I felt a small smile emerge from my incorporeal head-mate.

"Great! Well, stand up. At attention."

"This dancing or the army?"

"Both."

I stood up. "I hope this is some Earth dance."

"I've seen enough dancing in the moving pictures to know that our dances are very much alike."

I nodded.

"Let's start with a Court Stride. I think you call it a waltz. Put your arms up, as if you're holding onto someone."

I did so. Duer cocked his head. He was sitting on the rim of his birdhouse, watching. Toadstool growing must be getting boring.

"Not like that! You're not grappling undead, you're holding onto someone you're fond of. Left hand on their shoulder, lightly. Don't grab them. Yes, like that."

I bit my lip, resisting letting out a snarky reply. Usually, I would, but this was important.

"Other hand clasped in theirs, to the side. Good, like that."

I felt silly. My face must be red as a devil's. For once, I even cared what Duer thought of me. What was going through his little head right now? Couldn't stop now, though. I was too invested. Better finish up.

"Now, left foot back…"

Chapter 13. The Spectral Horseman

It became dark earlier this time of year, with the reddened sky turning to an earnest darkness around 6pm. It was winter after all. I hoped that the season wouldn't stop the ghost from falling for the trap. It shouldn't be a problem. Ghosts were simple creatures, if you looked past their typically difficult to set up exorcisms. They didn't have a concept of time. If they did, they wouldn't be haunting a place long past their death. It was their inability to let go of a certain event, at a certain time and place, that kept them on Earth and disturbing the living.

Well, that's what my research told me. I had come a long way from my hasty study of disturbances and spirits when I somehow exorcised the terror months before. Had read a lot of books since then. Even Treth took an interest. I think even he was tired of hunting walking corpses. Spirits were a good change of pace. Sure, they didn't fit into my usual M-O, but they were interesting. Required some creativity. It was nice to put my swords away once in a while. Metaphorically, of course. I still brought my swords. In a duffel bag, of course. I didn't need them for this hunt. Instead, I kept my holy salts, notes and purification apparatus in a small handbag (a loan from Trudie. She insisted that a backpack clashed with the dress).

Before leaving for the party, Trudie phoned to invite me to the Eternity Lounge. My date with Andy was the perfect excuse to get out of the simultaneously nerve-wracking and boring experience of clubbing. Trudie was so ecstatic that she even hung up without chewing my ear off for whatever reason. Practically screeched in excitement. Unfortunately for Pranish, he had no such excuse, and was being dragged along to the detestable club.

I arrived at the party by taxi soon after. Andy was to meet me there. Had business to attend to in Simon's Town, so was coming from completely the other direction. He lamented that he couldn't pick me up. But, it was fine. Really.

Tokai manor's lawn was lit up with fairy lights as cars parked around the circular road leading up to the house. The building itself was also lit up. It looked alive. Not that creepy, possessed house type of alive, but energetic. It was very different from my usual fare. I liked it.

I exited the taxi and waved him off. Was one of the regular drivers. Never caught his name. I was never typically in the mood to talk when in a taxi. I was normally sharpening my swords or covered in blood. This driver never questioned it. He was my favourite driver.

"Kat?"

I turned to see Andy, wearing a white dress shirt and black tie, approaching me and wearing a wide grin.

"Andy? You're here early."

He went in for a hug and I accepted it with some trepidation and genuine delight.

"You look good, Kat."

I hoped he couldn't see my blush in the light. I was wearing an identical dress to the one I had bought for the first failed date.

"Impressive what a good wash can do," he said.

"Or mass manufacturing. Makes replacing things super easy."

"Well, I'm glad I was able to see it in its proper colour. Red does look good on you, but I'd rather pass on the entrails."

I laughed and then presented my arm. Treth had made this part very clear.

"Let us go in."

He gave me an exaggerated bow and then grinned like a child. "It would be my privilege, my lady."

As we scaled the steps up to the manor's entrance, I couldn't help but give a faint smile.

"Enjoying yourself?" Treth asked. My smile disappeared. I liked Treth, but I hoped he wouldn't speak now. It felt like an invasion of my privacy – more so than when I went to the bathroom. It usually didn't matter, but tonight was different. I didn't feel like Treth coming along as a third-wheel. But at the same time, he had helped me prepare for this. And, he was kinda here to stay.

"Ms Drummond," Miriam said. "And her plus one…"

"Andy Garce," I said. "Andy, this is Miriam LeBlanc. The owner of the manor and our hostess."

"Garce? Related to Henry Garce?"

Andy nodded. "He is my father."

"Fascinating," Miriam replied, her tone revealing no scorn or genuine interest. I couldn't tell what she felt about the information. What I had learnt, however, was that

174

when someone said nothing, they probably only had bad things to say.

"I hope everything is ready for the exorcism, Ms Drummond," Miriam continued.

"If the party doesn't lure Frederick in, then I'll move onto plan B."

"Frederick?"

"The ghost's name."

"Oh, right. Forgot. Hard to think of it as having a name."

Miriam looked lost in thought. Andy and I remained standing by the doorway. A few guests were standing behind us.

Finally…

"Oh, yes. Please go right inside. I will be with you all shortly."

I bowed my head in thanks and we proceeded.

"Nice lady," Andy said.

I shrugged. A client is a client, and Miriam was friendly compared to many of them. Even if she wasn't, her contribution to vampiric lore gave her plenty of license to be a bit eccentric and rude.

We turned into the parlour, which was already filled with chattering guests. Peppering the wine glasses were beer bottles and tumblers of whisky. Miriam had a full bar running, equipped with its own black and white-clad bartender.

"Can I get you anything?" Andy asked.

I really wanted a scotch. But I never drank on the job, and this was a job.

"A coke, if they have it, please."

"Going cold turkey on me?" He grinned.

"Hah! Nah, just need my head in the game. You know? Spirits are tricky."

Andy nodded. I couldn't sense if he was disappointed, intrigued or…anything. Andy was a closed book. Very reserved. Perhaps that was what interested me. I sensed that he wanted to retrieve the drinks himself. A sort of chivalry sort of thing, so I waited as he went to the bar.

"You're smiling," Treth said.

I hadn't noticed, but I stopped.

"Nah, I like it. Seldom ever seen you smile that way. Always that feigned smile, or a grin at someone else's expense. Mostly, the undeads' expense. It's a welcome change."

I felt a bit irritable at Treth, but his comment also made me think. Did I really not smile? I thought I was happy. Well, happy-ish. I enjoyed my work. Had good friends. Had enough to eat. I must be happy!

Andy arrived back with two cans of coke. I raised my eyebrow quizzically.

"Designated driver," he said.

"I'm not drinking either."

"You can't drive."

"Oh, yeah."

A pause. Andy edged closer to me, and then looked at the dance floor. A few people were rocking side to side, but no dancing had started in earnest. I'm sure Miriam would enforce the activity later on. It was needed for the trap.

I took a sip of cola, masking the silence. Andy turned to me and was about to open his mouth when a man of about our age appeared like magic from behind us.

"Andy? Andy Garce?"

Andy frowned for a split second, but then put on a charming smile. I'd never seen someone change their expression so fast.

"Oliver! Fancy seeing you here."

"The same could be said of you. What got you off the computer and into your best suit?"

Andy indicated me. "Oliver, meet Kat. She is doing a job for the owner of the manor."

"Working with Ms LeBlanc?" he eyed me up and down. I felt like he was checking for fangs and pointy ears.

"Helping with renovations? Interior decorating?"

I shook my head and opened my mouth to speak.

"No, no. I got this. Event planning? Do we have you to thank for this party? Must say – it is class."

"I do not have the honour of being the event planner – no…"

"Kat is a monster hunter," Andy said. Oliver looked a bit disappointed that Andy had ruined the game, but then confused.

"Monsters?" He eyed me up and down. Looked at my arms for a bit.

"Well, got a nick here and there."

Andy opened his mouth, but Oliver threw him a stare. A serious one, unlike his previous demeanour. Andy's polite smile melted away.

"It's good you're here, Andy. I actually needed to talk to you."

"I know you don't care, Oliver, but I still have enough manners to not abandon my date."

I almost flushed at the last word.

Oliver spoke in a hushed tone. "It is about work. Won't take long. Can we speak outside?"

Andy clenched his fists. Subtly, but I noticed. He then unclenched them. "Fine. I'm sorry, Kat. Duty calls. I'll be back ASAP."

I nodded and tried to act cool. Wasn't a big deal. Andy and Oliver disappeared from the parlour.

"Abandoned so soon?" Miriam said, almost managing to sneak up on me. Fortunately, I heard her high-heels.

"He's a busy man," I said. "And always best to get things over and done with rather than sitting with the cloud of unfinished business."

"Wise," she said. "Wisdom brought about from experience?"

"I like to ensure my work is completed efficiently and on time. It is why people hire me."

"Of course. Do people only hire you for monster hunting?"

Small talk, or something deeper?

"Yes. I would say exclusively, but the types of hunts I take on range from straightforward extermination, to exorcisms such as this. Different approaches, but all under the same umbrella."

"And tell me, Ms Drummond, in all your hunts, have you ever faced a true vampire?"

Something deeper than small talk, my gut said.

"I have not. And while I am confident in my abilities, I don't think I'd be alive to tell you if I had."

Miriam's definition of true vampires was one that had not been turned by another vampire. That excluded ghouls, all lesser vampires and even most higher ones. True vampires were not cursed or infected beings. They were a species in their own right.

"I don't think all true vampires could match your combat prowess. They are a diverse breed. More diverse than I previously thought."

"New research?"

"Yes," Miriam said, as if stunned out of reverie. She must have been deep in contemplation. "For the new book."

"You mentioned something about rift-borne sites. On Robben Island, in particular."

I was referring to an island off the coast of Hope City. Pre-Cataclysm, it had been a prison for political dissidents. Post-Cataclysm, it started to experience weird rift surges. Wasn't a safe place to visit at the best of times.

"Have you ever heard of the Ancient Hypothesis?"

"Which one?" I asked, honestly. There were many with the same name.

"Vampiric lore."

I shook my head.

"It's a controversial theory. Most vampire specialists reject it. I did too but am beginning to give it a fair chance. You recall my summary in *Intro to Vampirism* on the mainstream theories of vampire origins?"

"Biological infection, a branch of necromancy or a complex curse, like lycanthropy."

Miriam nodded. "Exactly. But there's another origin theory. The Ancients."

A pause as Miriam sipped some red wine. I couldn't help but think she looked a bit like a vampire with the beverage in hand.

"The biological theory has no backing. Vampiric corpses, those that have been preserved, reveal no parasites, viruses, bacteria or such things in the specimen. The necromantic theory also doesn't hold up. While many vampires are adept necromancers, this is more due to the nature of dark beings using dark magic. And don't be confused, Ms Drummond. Despite my love for vampiric lore, I have very little love for vampires."

Well, that is good.

"But I do want to understand them. They are fascinating creatures. Alien, but not so. And every time I think I've solved a piece of the puzzle, it just gets muddled up again."

"Isn't it wisdom to know that we know nothing?"

"Paraphrasing Socrates?"

I grinned.

"Trite."

My grin faded.

"Back to the Ancients, Ms Drummond." She seemed really into the conversation now. "The only one of the mainstream theories that I believe still has any credence is that vampirism is a curse. But even so, it does not act like any other curse. It cannot be purified, for one. Even lycanthropy can be cured by skilled enough purifiers. But it is also undetectable by usual curse scanning methods."

"Then why think it is a curse?"

"A mark."

"Excuse me?"

"A mark. A scorched, albeit invisible, mark on the essential components of the vampire. In my tests, I have come to find this mark is consistent among vampires. In a way, it resembles weyline energy. Dark weyline energy, as is to be expected. Every vampire I have tested has this mark. It doesn't matter if a lesser turned animal or a higher true vampire."

The fact that Miriam had done her *test* on a higher true vampire was impressive and terrifying. I felt just a bit intimidated by this lady.

"What are the signs of a non-true vampire?" Miriam asked suddenly. I wracked my brain for that obscure titbit of knowledge.

"Bite scars are the easiest, but not always noticeable…"

"And some vampires don't need to bite their victims. But carry on…"

"If I recall, and it has been awhile, you argued that true vampires do not have the bloodlust. While it is still up for debate if they ever need to feed, they aren't as driven to do it."

"Exactly. And that has always been the essential difference between true and untrue vampires in our practical differentiation. It has also been the consensus that true vampires are the original vampires. And I believe it is true that true vampires were the first to come to our world, while I do believe many lesser vampires also came from the rifts. Nightkin, for example. But, I no longer believe that the true vampires are the original."

Miriam paused to let that proclamation set in. I leaned closer. I was completely enthralled. If only Miriam lectured my classes! I felt even Treth was completely consumed by the discussion.

"A true vampire's mark is darker than the rest. A blacker black. Lesser vampires have greyer, more translucent hues. It is as if they are diluted. But if they are diluted, where is the source? Where doth the water flow? The obvious answer is that the source are the true vampires. But, who created them? Who made them that way?"

A pause. She wanted me to reply.

"Did they have to be made? They could have evolved. A natural species that could then reproduce through infection."

"A worthy theory, and one I used to hold. But vampirism is more than just a species. It is imposed. It is alien even to the vampires themselves. That is why so many lesser vampires are deformed. It isn't meant to be there – vampirism, I mean. While it isn't a parasite, it acts like one. The mark imposes itself on the wearer, but not even that. It does something else. Something much more sinister."

Miriam leaned closer, as if she was giving me information that required extreme secrecy. I'd make sure to keep it.

"The mark is a fish hook, Ms Drummond. A siphon. A pipeline that defies the barriers in the same manner as the rifts. And if it is a pipeline…it has to go somewhere."

"Excuse me…" The voice and hand on my shoulder shook me out of my enthrallment. I almost leapt into a defensive stance. Miriam seemed unfazed. She took a long sip from her glass.

"I'm back," Andy said. "Apologies for interrupting."

"It is quite alright, Mr Garce," Miriam said. "Let me not keep your lady any longer. She will need to be getting to work soon, anyway."

She sniffed. "I feel a spectral glow on the horizon."

She walked off. Andy looked at me questioningly. I shrugged.

"Brilliance requires eccentricity."

He laughed.

"How did your chat with Oliver go?"

"Fine. He's freaking out about nothing. Deadlines and all that."

"May I ask of the nature of your business with him?"

"A bit nosey…"

"Comes with the job."

186

"Thought you said you weren't a detective. You kept repeating it last time we went to the Gravekeeper – three pints in."

I crossed my arms. Andy chuckled.

"Fine. Let's trade. I'll tell you about my business, if you give me the honour of a dance."

I noticed now that the dance floor had begun filling up with slow dancers. A live band of all sorts of instruments were egging them on. Miriam must have been doing well for herself to afford all this. I wonder how. Academia didn't pay that well. Especially if you refused to work through mainstream academia.

Andy presented his arm. I reached for it, hesitated, smiled, and accepted.

He led me to the dance floor and began leading. I was thankful for that. I found out after Treth's lesson that he'd only taught me how to do the follower part of the waltz. We did a few steps and as the live band quietened, preparing to transition to the next song...

"Deal is a deal, Mr Garce. What's your business?"

"IT."

I looked at him dully. He grinned mischievously.

"What did you expect?"

"Spying for the Magocracy, dealing in illegal tomes, ogre trafficking...you know, something interesting."

"So, you're saying you'll only find me interesting if I'm a criminal?"

"Not at all..."

The live band resumed in earnest. A slower song. Melodic. Andy leaned in closer, and I did the same. I felt heat resonate from him. Smelled his cologne. Felt every part of skin that touched his, bare or through our clothes.

"I already find you interesting," I finished.

Andy looked at me, deep into my eyes, and I looked back. My heart beat fast. Fear? No, not fear. Something. A curse? No. Not that.

"Close your eyes," Treth said.

Who was he trying to lecture?!

But I closed my eyes.

Then, a neigh. I opened my eyes. The lights had been shut off, and a green-white glow shone through the curtained windows. The neighing continued, growing more feverish and demented. And with it, laughing and weeping simultaneously.

It didn't sound human, yet it was so eerily human.

I looked at Andy, barely illuminated by the ghostly glow. My look must have said more than words ever could, as he nodded and let go. I ran out the parlour, pulling open the front door and being greeted, just a metre away, by a mounted man wearing a dishevelled 19th century jacket and undershirt, stained with blood and booze. His horse was simultaneously flesh and skeleton, with twisted and smashed bone poking out from its legs. They were translucent, but opaque enough for me to make out the details. He was cleanshaven. Young. My age, about it. He had bags under his eyes. Worse than mine. It was as if he hadn't slept for centuries. He hadn't.

The ghost, and I had to resist covering my ears. It was as if a wind tunnel had been put up to my ears, and then filled with the mourning of a thousand funerals. It was a bellow, a deep and sorrowful cry that could never be uttered by a human yet felt so deeply human. It was that primal cry that all that have lost something want to call out but cannot.

The cry abated, and the horseman stared at me. My heart was pounding.

"It can't hurt you," Treth yelled. He did that when on the hunt, even if he didn't need to. I liked it. It helped put me back on track.

I heard footsteps and gasps behind me. The party had come for the show. Well, it was time to give them one.

I reached into Trudie's purse, slowly, and drew out a vial of fine powder. An elvish script rune was engraved on the glass. I wasn't a wizard, but there was a first time for everything, and the weyline here was very strong. I just hoped Pranish's tutelage would be enough.

"Raz…"

Just the simple uttering of the word of power, still not even a complete spell, sent a feeling of power throughout my core and veins. Every syllable. Every letter. Power. The vial warmed in my hand, and the spirit horse stamped its hoof, uncomfortable.

"Gy," I continued. With the next, the power felt even more focused. More bound to my will. With that will, I aimed it at the vial in my hand and at the spirit before me.

"Eraz!"

I finished the simple exorcism spell with a crescendo and a throw of the vial. Usually, nothing could touch an ethereal spirit. And ghosts were very much ethereal. But this purifying vial of holy salt no longer cared about such petty principles. It burst on impact, and the ghost shrieked. Its horse bucked with a screech. I pressed the attack and surged forward, tossing an arc of loose holy salt mixed with silver flakes at it. I was rewarded with a hiss.

This was the force side of exorcism.

"Frederick Eksteen!" I shouted. The ghost's head pivoted towards me.

This was the persuasion part.

"Your time is done, Frederick. You no longer belong to this world. Any unfinished business you have, shall remain unfinished."

The ghost wailed at me. Incomprehensible. I waited for its tirade to end. The horse bucked again, its back legs passing over the half-wall that it had leapt over to its death 200 years ago.

"You stand now at your place of death, Frederick…"

Repeating its name apparently helped with the exorcism. Well, according to *Intros to Exorcism* and *Spirit Smashing 101*. Something about grounding the spirit in reality.

I threw some more salt at it and approached closer, and closer. It backed away. Another torrent of salt. Smoke and hissing. And then it jumped off the building.

All according to plan.

I rushed down the steps, careful not to slip and meet a similar fate to Frederick.

"Do not try running, Fred! You cannot escape what happened. You cannot change it. Do not hurt yourself anymore."

The spirit stood astride his equally spectral horse, in the centre of his lawn. He was surrounded by cars. He stood upright. In a way, noble. Defiant. But I could smell the booze washing off him. I could see his sadness. His trauma. All ghosts had something to hold them back. The act of exorcism was making that thing irrelevant.

"Catherine is no longer here, Fred."

He didn't move and neither did his horse. I approached, walking. I didn't throw any more salt. I walked right up to the spirit, only a few feet away. I felt the stares of the party-goers on my back. Andy would be among them.

I looked into the spirits eyes, and he stared back.

Was this Frederick Eksteen?

The horse turned its head and looked at me as well.

It could be Frederick. But how could a ghost from almost 200 years before the Cataclysm exist? How could a spirit survive without any of the essential magic that now seeped into our world?

And did it matter?

There was a ghost before me. It could be Frederick. It could be some rift-wrought spirit from another realm. But it didn't matter. It was tied here by a story. An earthly narrative about a boy who'd died. A boy with unfinished business that could never truly be finished. You could never really help a spirit by settling the unsettled. How could you? They were dead, and the dead cannot finish what they left undone.

"Go," I said simply and quietly.

The night went dark as the ghost disappeared. Silent. It would be silent for every night since. The spectral horseman no longer haunted these estates and woods. And he never would again.

Chapter 14.   Relationships

Andy dropped me off at home after the party in his Mercedes. We didn't speak on the way. Just a quick "Congratulations" from him for finishing the hunt, and then a long and dark drive home. Miriam had been pleased, at least. She said she'd pay Conrad and ensure I got my cut. Also said I could contact her to talk about vampires anytime. I had smiled, faintly. I did appreciate it. I ran into vamps often in my line of work and having her consulting would save me a lot of time in the archives. I was tired, though. Physically, and emotionally. I didn't know why. Wasn't a strenuous hunt by any stretch. Sure, Frederick's story was a moving one, and I even felt a bit sad for him, but I had gone through worse. Then what was it that had tired me out?

As Andy stopped outside my apartment complex, I half expected him to lean over and kiss me. Instead, he stopped the car, got out and opened the door for me. All gentlemanly like.

"Thanks for the invite, Kat," he said.

"Sorry for the disruption," I mumbled, avoiding eye-contact.

"It's fine. I knew what I was getting into when I asked you out the first time."

I frowned. I didn't think he truly knew what he was getting into.

"Well, good night, Kat."

He got back into his car. No hug. No kiss. I waved him off, nonchalantly, but as he passed around the corner, I stomped down hard and swore loudly.

"I thought that went well," Treth said.

I grumbled in response and made my way to my apartment. Both Alex and Duer greeted me at the door, the novelty of my arrival establishing a temporary treaty between the two rivals.

"How'd it go?" Duer squeaked. Alex meowed, as if asking the same question.

"Duer…" I started, placing my bag down. "How do I know if a boy likes me?"

"Well, if I liked someone, I'd give them flower petals. If I really liked them, I'd share my honey and vodka with them. But that's only if I really liked them."

"Is that what you did with your family?"

"Every day," Duer said, seriously. "Good night, Kat."

Well, that wasn't much help. I bent down to stroke Alex. The cat purred and snaked his way around my legs.

I really wished that the ghost hadn't interrupted Andy and me...

"I'm pretty sure Andy likes you, Kat," Treth said.

I stood up to open a can of cat food for Alex. Treth continued.

"He's made it pretty clear. Men are simple creatures. When we're as open as he is, it means we are confident about our feelings."

"Really?" I said, a hint of vulnerability in my voice that I kicked myself for.

"Really. Andy wouldn't have asked to court you if he didn't like you. And he accepted the second date after the problem with the mimic."

"I know, but I can't help but feel that I screwed up tonight..."

I sat down on the couch with a heavy oomph. Alex ate his canned food greedily and I heard Duer's faint snores from the birdhouse. I envied his ability to fall asleep so quickly and soundly.

"The moment was perfect." I sighed. "And then that damn ghost had to come ruin it all. Murphy's law. Just my damn luck."

"He doesn't seem like the type of guy to change his entire view on something like that."

"I don't think we know him well enough to say that…"

I hesitated. I had said "we". As if Treth was in this as well. And I remembered the irritation I had held for him earlier. That I had wanted him away. Not forever, but just for that moment. But Treth couldn't go away. He was a part of me. Like it or not, we were both in this. But was that fair on him?

Treth sighed, heavily. One of his rare sighs. It was one of those times he truly sounded human. Exasperated. Not just a spirit or figment of my twisted mind.

"Kat, there are things more important than the quest."

"Never thought I'd hear you say something like that." I wanted to snicker but couldn't. I reclined on my couch, sinking deeper into the upholstery.

"Quests aren't good for their own sake. They exist for something greater. To protect people. To find meaning. To find love. We're stuck together, Kat, but I don't want that to mean that you don't get to have a life. That you don't get to find love. Andy may or may not be the one, but I want you to find that out for yourself. We can make my toilsome existence work. Love is too important to let quests or pesky spirits get in its way."

I frowned. "Are you sure, Treth?"

"Hey. It's your body."

I smiled faintly but genuinely. "Thanks, Treth."

I stood up, reinvigorated enough to take care of my pre-sleep activities. I then slumped into bed, too tired to read but too awake to fall asleep. So, instead, I contemplated. Contemplated love. Contemplated the night. Contemplated Andy. And thought about what it all meant alongside my *raison d' être*, my quest to hunt monsters. Could I make it work? And was it really fair on Treth if I did it? He didn't strike me as the voyeur type. Sure, he liked watching mundane things. But...

I didn't really know my spirit head-mate as well as I should.

"Treth," I finally whispered."

"What, Kat?"

"Have you ever been in love?"

Hesitation. And then a quick, "Yes."

It was the type of curt response that asked me not to pry any further on that topic. I've never been one for obedience.

"What about sex?"

"Go to sleep, Kat."

With a mischievous grin, I finally drifted off to sleep.

***

I awoke with that terrible feeling that workaholics get when they don't have anything to do. I had been preparing for the spectral horseman case for a while, and the mimic hunt beforehand. It had been a while since I had been truly work-free, and it disturbed me. While I may complain about work on occasion, I complained even more when I didn't have any. I needed to go see Conrad to get another job, but unfortunately it was a Sunday. Even the money-grabbing Mr Khoi took a day off.

So, rather than the more understandable and quantifiable affairs of monster hunting, I thought of the more angst-ridden and eternally unsolvable issues of relationships.

Was Andy upset about what happened? And if so: was he upset enough to give up on me? Was there anything I could do about it?

"You've usually gobbled your noodles up by now…" Treth said.

I grunted in reply. Not aggressively or derisively. Half-heartedly. My head was not in the game. Well, there was no game. That was a part of the problem. Games had rules. They had parameters. In general, everyone knew what the rules were. And the rules didn't change. Relationships? That was a whole different issue.

"What's the plan for today?" Treth asked.

I didn't reply. I continued to poke my noodles. Was spicy ramyun flavour. Was hoping the heat would wake me up from this funk.

Come on, Kat! I told myself. *Stop moping and do something.*

Do something?

"What could I do?" I said aloud.

"Make the first move. Take the initiative," Treth said.

"Hunting strategy?"

"Works as well."

I tightened my grip on my fork.

Yeah. The initiative. And this time, nothing to get in the way. No jobs to draw me away. A relaxed Sunday…

I reached for my cell phone on the countertop. I'd phone Andy. Would ask him if we could finish where we'd left off last night. A nice Sunday date…

My phone rang. A bzzzt bzzzt as I hadn't taken it off silent.

The caller ID said Pranish. I'd have to let him down easily. Would thank him for the spell but refuse any activities he wanted to do today. I needed today for dating.

"Hey, Pranish…" I began.

"Kat!" he said, his voice resonating with an anxiety I hadn't heard since I'd saved him from a poltergeist.

"What is it, Pranish?"

"She…she didn't answer. Thought she'd be fine by herself. I didn't know. I couldn't."

"Who didn't answer? What has happened?" I kept my voice calm but let through just a hint of anger. I'm a bit impatient, as you may have guessed.

"Trudie's gone missing. There…there was some sort of attack at the club. She's…Trudie's gone."

I almost dropped the phone.

"Hello?" Pranish said, as I didn't reply.

I rubbed my chin with my free hand. Took a deep breath. And then spoke as calmly as I could.

"Come pick me up. Take me to the club."

I must have sounded awfully scary, as Pranish hung up immediately. I hoped he'd remember to lock his front door. For all that was worth.

"A few minutes to get dressed," I said. I was still in my pyjamas. Comfortable t-shirt and sleeping shorts. I could keep the shirt on. Didn't exactly care about fashion at this very moment.

"You'll need your strength," Treth said, probably indicating my unfinished food.

"No time. And lost my appetite."

He nodded.

"What are you going to do?"

"I'm not a detective," I said. "But I'm a hunter. And if that means hunting down a friend to make sure she's safe, then I'm sure I can adjust."

Chapter 15.   The Eternity Lounge

I was on the curb with my full monster hunting kit when Pranish came screeching around the corner, jolting to a halt. Ms Ndlovu was just outside, exterminating weeds, and looked like she was about to shout bloody murder at Pranish. The look on both our faces made her reconsider.

"What happened? Exactly, and comprehensibly, please," I asked Pranish after I sat down, and he did a swift U-turn back up the street.

"Trudie took us to the Eternity Lounge."

"You and her?"

"And one of her new friends. Girl named Stephanie. Was the usual. Loud music, overly sweet alcohol…"

"The point, Pranish."

"Sorry…I left early. Thought Stephanie and Trudie could chaperone each other. They're adults. But…I got a feeling in my gut this morning that something was up. I phoned Trudie and her cell went straight to voice mail. Phoned her parents. They hadn't seen her. Thought she was staying over with me or you. And then, I phoned the lounge…"

Pranish screeched to a halt at a red light, the nose of the car very much over the line. He tapped his fingers impatiently and anxiously.

"What did they say?"

"They didn't answer either…"

I didn't blame Pranish for his temperament now. I had a bad feeling about this.

"So, we're headed to the Eternity Lounge?"

Pranish nodded.

The light went green and Pranish sped off like a rally driver.

***

The Eternity Lounge was cordoned off by red and blue tape. Puretide. Must be the building's paranormal security agency of choice. I didn't exactly dislike the agency. They did good work. Sure, they were my competition, but that hadn't ever really affected me. I was a small-timer. Couldn't be expected to wrestle a hundred-zombie strong horde or higher vampire. Even so, their presence at the Eternity Lounge made me the most uneasy I had been in ages.

Pranish parked his car haphazardly near a Puretide van. Wasn't technically legal, but we weren't much in the mood for traffic regulations or the ire of mega-agencies. Worst that could happen is they get us to move.

I exited the car as a guy wearing a Puretide combat vest came towards us. His irritated expression turned to surprise as he recognised me.

"Drummond?"

I nodded, stiffly.

"Why is head office hiring freelancers? We can handle this!"

I didn't know the guy, but he knew me. Conrad was right. I had a reputation.

"This isn't official. My friend was last seen in the club. What happened?"

His face went grim. He avoided my eyes.

"I'm sorry, Drummond. We got the call out at 4am. Alarm went off but when we got here, the place was empty. No signs of struggle. Still doing the magic tests. Also testing for a reverse rift."

My heart skipped a beat. A reverse rift was technically just a rift. But instead of spitting monsters and magic into our world, it sucked in Earth things and spat them somewhere else. Nobody who had gone through a rift had ever returned to their world. We didn't even know if any of them survived. I must have let my horror show, as the Puretide guy raised his palms up.

"No need to freak out. All the furniture and drinks are still in there, so pretty sure it wasn't a rift."

Freak out? I wasn't freaking out. Or was I? I did breathe a sigh of relief. A rift would suck in everything, like a blackhole.

"Any suspicions?"

"That's kinda classified." He squirmed. I approached him closer. He glanced down at the hilts of my dual dusacks. I ignored the handle of his .45.

"I'm not competing for the cash here. My friend was in there. This is personal."

"Still, I could get fired – unless you're brought on the case. If you get the okay from HQ, then you can do what you want."

I spun on my heels and walked away from the guy. I didn't blame him for not caving. I wasn't at my peak level intimidation today. Pranish was still sitting in the car, hands still on the wheel. I leant through his window. He was muttering to himself. I grabbed his shoulder and he jumped.

Seeing that it was me, he calmed. "I shouldn't have left her, Kat. We both know how she acts. Mothering everyone else, but no concern for her own safety."

"Isn't anything you could have done. You stayed, and I'd be having to track both you and her."

He nodded, but I detected that he was unsatisfied. He felt responsible. Damn the logic. Was a man thing. Didn't matter if he couldn't have done anything. All that mattered was that he didn't. Powerlessness was not something anyone wanted to feel.

I stood up from the window and leant against the car, facing the club. Puretide forensics guys were going in and out. A guy in combat gear was smoking with a cop. The guy I had spoken to before joined them.

Every second they wasted on this routine investigation that they didn't personally care about was a second, I could be tracking down and saving Trudie from whatever worldly or other-worldly thing had got to her.

I drew my phone as I would a knife and dialled Conrad.

"Kat? It's Sunday. I don't work on Sundays."

"Mass disappearance by the Eternity Lounge in Old Town. Puretide has the place cordoned off."

"Why should we care?"

"My friend was in there. The goth."

A pause. I continued.

"I want to be put on the case."

"It'll be hard, Kat. And not much money. Not really sure it's worth it."

"My friend is missing, Conrad. I don't care about the fucking money."

A pause, and a sigh. "I'll see what I can do, but don't hold your breath. Gonna take a lot of string pulling. A lot of favours…"

"Kat?"

I turned, and standing before me was Andy, dressed in a fleecy hoodie and jeans. I suppressed my surprise as best I could and pointed to my phone. He spoke anyway.

"No need to pull strings. Already done. I got my dad to give us carte blanche inside."

The shock lasted a second, and then I said to Conrad. "Never mind. Got a way in."

"Good luck, Kat. And don't waste your entire Sunday."

I put my phone back in my pocket and turned to Andy.

"How'd you hear?"

"Knew Trudie was at the Eternity Lounge last night. Also knew she missed the deadline for our group project today. Didn't pick up her phone, so knew something was up. Had a gut feeling you'd be here, so got my dad to push through a warrant."

I raised my eyebrow. Seemed a bit odd, but this was an odd town.

"Thanks. Do you have it?"

"Yep." He withdrew a sheet of paper with a lawmantic sigil emblazoned across it. A truly powerful piece of paper. If Puretide disobeyed it, they'd be violating the highest laws of the State of Good Hope.

I put my hand out to take it. Andy pulled it back. I noticed a slightly amused grin. Was this a game?

"I'm coming in too. You'll need a second pair of eyes."

What did he hope to achieve? He wasn't a detective. Wasn't even a monster hunter. All he would do was distract me. Slowly, the warmth I had felt for him began to cool. Just a tad. But he was just trying to help. I couldn't let my anger at this case affect my view of him.

"Fine," I conceded. "Let's go."

The same Puretide guy from before tried to stop us at the tape, but a read-through over the warrant let us through. The Puretide forensics guys even left to give us run of the place.

I had only been to the Eternity Lounge once before. It looked very different then. Had been flooded with people, pulsing with flashing lights and filled with ear-splitting music. Now, it was quiet and empty. It's usually closed blinds from some high up windows were open, letting in natural light that pooled on the black-painted concrete floors.

It wasn't a big club. It just felt big when an ocean of people inhabited it. Now, with only me and Andy inside, it was much smaller than the Gravekeeper. A cramped dance floor was located in a sunken part of the floor, with a DJ booth just above it. All the DJ equipment, some of it costing more than my net worth, was still located where it had been left last night. Up from the dance floor, a cramped floor at street-level culminated in a crescent shaped purple bar. Half-drunk glasses and bottles covered the table top. Notes and coins of all denominations were strewn between puddles of liquor and cigarette ash. It was as if someone was passing the money to another when both just disappeared.

"Doesn't look like a robbery," Andy said. "Too many valuables left behind."

He bent down to examine a broken beer bottle. Wasn't necessarily from a struggle. Drunk people kind of forgot about bins. I proceeded without a word, looking for…anything.

But there was nothing to indicate this was my type of case. No scratch marks. No blood. No damage besides the usual you'd find in a sketchy bar.

"It's as if they've been raptured," I said.

"Excuse me?"

"Raptured. Moved on. Like the end of the world has come and we've been left behind."

I looked at an empty barstool that I imagined Trudie sitting at.

"Never imagined Trudie'd be one to go up, though."

"Didn't know you were Christian," Andy said, sidling up to me. I don't know why, but I unconsciously shifted a centimetre away.

"I'm not. Well, I was raised Christian. But things change."

I shrugged. Andy must have sensed that I was not in any sort of amiable mood and backed away a bit.

"I'm going to go take a look around. Maybe see if there's something in the back."

I nodded. When he was around the corner, Treth spoke.

"This is odd, Kat."

Didn't need to nod. He continued.

"It's not humans. At least, not non-magic users. Not any monster we've dealt with before."

I sighed. "What do we have to go on, Treth?"

He paused, thinking. My heart was beating anxiously. Trudie... Trudie was out there. Somewhere. Hopefully not dead yet.

"Close your eyes. Focus. See if the weyline has been tampered with."

"The Puretide guys would have tested the weyline already."

"Weyline corruption can be hidden. You know this as well as I do. But the feeling of unease cannot be masked. If as dark a magic as I suspect has been used here, then there will be a trace."

I closed my eyes and, for a while, only felt the warm sun heating my nape through the small window. We had done this before. It was not exactly a science, but Treth and I could often get a good handle of a place's magical energy through some low-key meditation.

"Reach out, Kat…"

"I am, I am…"

Nothing. Nothing. And then something. Faint. Like seeing footprints in the sand, but far away. With my eyes still closed, I walked towards it, and it grew stronger. And with every step, I grew colder and my heart beat faster. I walked into a barstool and over some glass. I felt the glass embedded in my shoes weigh it down. They'd survived worse.

I stopped, suddenly.

"You feel it?" Treth asked.

"Yes." Of course, I did! How could anyone not. It was like a huge gaping wound, wheezing out pus-filled air. That is a disgusting metaphor. But best I could do.

I opened my eyes. I had made it to the far side of the room. Bathrooms and the fire escape were ahead.

"Dark magic," Treth said. "And we've felt it before."

"Yes…"

But where? I clicked my fingers as I remembered.

"The mimic!"

"Exactly. Didn't think it was magic then. Just its odour," Treth said. "But it is unmistakable. Something that had clung to the mimic was here. Something malicious."

"So, killing the mimic wasn't the end of it?"

"Seems that way. It seems your suspicions were true, Kat. Something bigger is afoot."

"And Trudie has been caught in the middle of it."

I clenched my fist. My friend had been made victim in some sick fuck's game. I'd make them pay.

"Let's see if Andy has found anything."

I made my way into the back. Didn't hear Andy, so opened the first door – the male bathroom. Empty. But smelled disgusting. I hastily closed it and checked the female bathroom. No people, but streaks of white powder on the countertops. I showed my disgust. It wasn't that I was anti-drugs, it was just that I tended to not like the types of people who took drugs. Stereotypes exist for a reason and druggies were a pretty negative stereotype. I closed the door and proceeded to the back office.

The back-office door was closed. Red door with aluminium cladding on the top and bottom. No handle. One of those push doors. I pushed it open to reveal a dank and dark room. It was smaller than Conrad's. Filing cabinets lined the back wall, crammed fill of crumpled pieces of paper. Dominating the centre of the room was a metal desk with an old PC. No Andy.

"Andy?" I called.

I heard a rattle, a clank, and Andy appeared from underneath the desk.

"What were you doing under there?"

"Looking for clues."

"And?"

He shook his head, frowning.

"Shit, well. I think we've seen all that we can here. Need to do some research."

Andy stood up, dusted himself off and left the room. I turned to leave but felt something. A tug. Like a cold, small hand reaching towards me. I'd tell anyone else who felt such a tug to run as fast as they could. But that's cause they're not a professional. I am. And these sorts of tugs are my bread and butter. I walked to the desk and bent down where Andy had been hiding just before. The ground was empty. Just some lint and cigarette butts. Despite the dirt, I touched the ground and heard my own heartbeat. Icicles went up my bones.

Unmistakable. Necromantic energy residue. I knew its cold, deathly feel better than any other magic. This wasn't strong. Anyone unused to it would just think there were bad vibes. The culprit must have tried to coat over the casting with some cloaking spells but failed to hide it all.

Was a necromancer responsible for all this? And if so: how long did Trudie have before she became a wight, an abhorrent or a zombie?

I perished the thought. It wouldn't help me. I'd get to that dreadful possibility when it became necessary.

"Kat?" Andy asked, leaning into the room.

"I'm coming."

We exited the club and I got Pranish to drive me home. I didn't care if Andy was offended that I had rejected his offer of a lift. I needed to think, and Andy was too distracting. And no longer just as someone I held affection for.

Chapter 16.   Darkness

After fruitlessly interviewing the Puretide investigators and possible witnesses, I spent the rest of the day feverishly going through every bit of relevant news, hunter gossip and mish-mashed paranormal research I could find. This took me hours upon hours. Hours that I didn't eat, or even drink. I only stopped once to go to the bathroom and continued my research while there on my cell. My research took me well into the night. There was so much to go through. Mimics. Necromancers. Disappearance magic. And real disappearances. So many disappearances. Before and after I had slain the mimic. My lounge became strewn with my notes. I had stuck up many on the windows, including a graph showing reported disappearances by day. After the elimination of the mimic, there was an unmistakable decline in disappearances. But it was up again and, with the events at the Eternity Lounge, it was soaring to new heights. Fifty people had gone poof late at night, without a trace. That was cause for concern. Fact that the City wasn't doing anything about it made it even worse.

Tens, if not hundreds, of people, had disappeared without a trace. Even in a city filled with monsters, this was unusual. Monsters left a lot of blood. But this...this left nothing. And that was why I felt hopeless. No tracks. No trace of the victim or their killer. No indication that there was anyone killed in the first place. At least with the mimic case, I had some sort of lead. Drake had done most of the work for me. As I kept reminding myself, I'm no detective. I'm a stupid monster hunter. A blunt instrument. And while this hadn't mattered much in the past, I always managed to get by in the end, I truly felt despair now. My friend was in trouble, and I couldn't do anything about it.

I worked for an age, but even as my eyes blurred from staring at screen and paper for so long, I didn't feel I knew any more than before.

"Rift-dammit, Trudie..." I said aloud, looking over the disappearances graph again, looking for some pattern. My eyes had moistened over the past while, but I always kept the frustrated tears at bay.

"We'll find her," Treth said.

I didn't have his confidence. How could I? I didn't know anything. I felt I knew even less than when I had started the research.

My stomach rumbled.

"You need to eat," Treth said, his voice filled with real concern.

I reached for my phone to check another news site, to see if the cops had taken an interest at all when the hunger pangs hit me and became too much. I imagined this is what zombies must feel like all the time. Felt a bit sorry for them. Only a bit.

"Fine," I said, and made my way to my minuscule kitchen adjoined to the lounge area.

I didn't have much in stock. I didn't feel like making anything. Was too tired. So, I just put some bread into a toaster paid for by a now very dead lesser vampire mutt. I sat down to wait for the toast to pop.

I didn't know I had nodded off until I was woken up by the simultaneous pop of the toast and my phone ringing. Both sounds shook me wide awake, placing me firmly into a state of blurry confusion. I took a few rapid breaths, and then reached for my phone, ignoring the toast. I had the small hope that it'd be Trudie on the phone, telling me all was well. But the number was unknown. It didn't even show the digits. Caller ID withheld and all that. I grimaced. I hated people like that. Mostly scammers and telemarketers.

It continued to ring, and my irritation turned to curiosity. Nobody called at this time. Even telemarketers. It was nearing midnight. What could it be?

And then I felt a strong unease. Nobody called this time of night. Only few people were awake at this time. People like me, and the people I hunted.

Despite my better judgement, I answered.

The phone was filled with a loud static. Not that low-pitched hiss from a bad line, but a deep rumble. I heard deep breathing on the other side, obscured by a voice modulator.

"Hello?" I said.

"Hello, Kat," the voice answered, deep as a mineshaft and sounding like a storm cloud. It sent chills down my spine. I considered hanging up there and then, but I'm no coward.

"Who is this?" I asked, rallying the most confident voice I could.

"That is unimportant, Kat." The way the voice said my name made me want to crumple into a ball. "What is important, is the fate of your friend."

"Listen here, fucker!" All fear gone, I started shouting. Nobody hurts my friends, and nobody uses my friends against me! "You touch a hair on my friend's head and I'll end you."

"I do not have the privilege of Trudie's company, Kat. What I do have, however, is information."

"You know where she is?" I was still fuming but shifted my tone at the proclamation. Was in full instinct mode now. Needed to do whatever it took.

"I do."

"Tell me!"

"You like trade, don't you Kat?"

I didn't answer. Didn't know what my views on economics had to do with this.

"Let's do a trade. A favour for a favour."

I paused. A favour...for this human or creature? I'd have to be insane. But Trudie...

"What favour?"

"I will give you the information you need to save your friend, and others. In exchange, you will ignore a call-out. Your boss will be phoning you any minute. You will not answer the phone."

I opened my mouth to speak.

"I'll know. And besides, you're on a timer. Can't work and pick up the information. So, you have a choice. What will it be? The job, or your friend's life?"

"Where is the info?" I answered, without hesitation. The thought of working with this unknown horror made me feel sick, but my friend came first.

"You're predictable, Kat. I like that. You can pick up the info at the corner of Florence and Wrensch streets. It will be stuck underneath a bench."

I was about to hang up. The voice spoke again.

"Don't double-cross me, Kat. I'll know."

I hung up.

***

I really should have called a taxi, but I wasn't thinking straight. All I knew is that I had an address. A lead.

Something that could lead me to Trudie and whatever or whoever was keeping her.

I ignored the incessant phone calls from Conrad, as ordered. It was very unlike him to phone at this time. And it was even more unlike me to not pick up. But I couldn't answer them even if I was allowed to. I was running full sprint down the streets of Hope City, towards Florence and Wrensch. My lungs burned from the exertion as I didn't let up my full sprint.

I knew roughly where the streets were. I travelled the city a great deal in my line of work and got to learn a lot of street names and neighbourhoods. Sometimes, I had to give directions to the normally street-savvy taxi drivers who often shipped me place to place. Florence Avenue and Wrensch Road were near the disused train tracks in Observatory. A little bit further north than the Gravekeeper. Wasn't a bad neighbourhood. I did a lot of work in its only semi-decaying streets. At least the creepy voice hadn't told me to go delving into the slums.

I collapsed in a heap as I reached Rosebank. I had been running for what seemed like hours. As I breathed and tried not to vomit, I checked my phone and realised it had been almost half an hour. I wasn't even halfway there. I also had forty-three missed calls.

A timer, the voice had said. I had a limited time to get there.

Rift-dammit, Kat. Get yourself together! Your friend needs you to be cooler than normal, not less.

I had caught a bit of my breath back and went to speed dial the taxi service.

"No taxies available. Apologies for the inconvenience."

Fucking typical. Always at the worst time.

I looked up from my phone. I was standing on the sidewalk of a pretty fat roadway. It was usually bustling, but at this time of night, there was no one. I heard some traffic on the freeway in the distance, but this was ultimately a suburban road – despite its size. No soccer moms ferrying their kids around at this time. At least the street lights were on.

I felt a bit uneasy. Quiet streets that were usually loud. Quietly flickering streetlights. Was just like my encounter with the cloaked figure at North Road, months ago. I'd been strangled by dark magic then. I had thought that the cloaked figure was the necromancer I was being paid to track down, but I had been wrong. I still knew nothing about them, and the only man who could have possibly told me anything had been eviscerated by my knife.

"How far is it?" Treth asked.

"Very far." I scowled, and then my lip quivered. No, Kat. This isn't the time. But how was I going to get there? I couldn't run all night. And I was being weighed down by my gear.

"What if…" Treth began, and then stopped.

"What if what?" I then noticed what he'd seen. A bicycle, shoddily chained to a street-side bench.

"No, Treth. We aren't thieves."

"Desperate times, Kat. And you can return it on the way back."

I glowered, wrinkling my forehead. I'm not a thief, but if I'm just borrowing…

"Fine."

The bike's lock was easy to break. I just put it between the concrete edge of the bench and bludgeoned it with the butt of my sword until it fell away. Easy. Didn't feel great, though. A person's property was everything. I'd have to make sure to get the bike back in one piece.

Illuminated streets turned to darkness, as I rode down suburban roads that hadn't been serviced in decades. I seldom rode a bicycle, and the going was tough, but I soon got into the rhythm and found myself in the scarcely lit intersection of Florence and Wrensch. I'd crossed over the tracks onto Florence a while back. A benefit of a lack of trains meant no fences to stop people from crossing the tracks. The intersection was lit by a single yellow streetlight, hanging over a concrete and decaying wooden bench. Behind the bench was an overgrown field. Unsold or abandoned property. Some fallen wire mesh was pressed into the ground and as I approached the bench, I could see a sun-faded "For Sale" sign. I shook my head. It was a shame. Such prime real estate left unsold just because it didn't have a weyline. So many perfectly usable properties were left to rot just because of a lack of magical energy. It's not like everyone needed magic. Plenty of people used magical appliances, but you didn't have to. I didn't, for instance. Got along just fine without them.

I parked the bike next to a telephone pole opposite the bench. Didn't know why, exactly. It just felt like I should keep it away from the bench. That the bench was a battleground and if I wanted the bicycle to come off unscathed, I needed to keep it at a distance. I dismounted my *borrowed* bicycle and crossed the street. It had been raining lightly, and my shoes squelched on the tarmac. As I reached the bench, I realised that I had unconsciously drawn my sword. You could say I was on edge.

Under the bench, the voice had said.

I squatted, and put my free hand underneath the bench, feeling for something stuck there.

"Kat…" Treth said, his voice wary.

I stood up and jumped. Looked around. Nothing.

"In the tree."

I looked up.

It was faint. A muddled shadowy figure in an equally shadowy tree. But the moon and streetlight threw just enough light to reveal a crow perched on the leafless tree, staring at me. But it wasn't just any crow. It had one eye, and an exposed ribcage.

An undead.

My breath caught in my throat as I realised what I had just done. Who I had been speaking to. That voice on the phone. It had been a necromancer. I was doing the bidding of a necromancer. I had ignored Conrad's calls. I dreaded speaking to him again. But more than that, I dreaded hearing about what I had failed to do. I clenched my hand over my sword-hilt.

After I found Trudie, someone would pay.

I looked away from the crow. If it hadn't attacked me already, it wasn't going to attack at all. It was a flesh puppet. Its owner probably had its other eye set up in some necromantic contraption linked to an old PC monitor. Surveillance.

I knelt down again and felt underneath the bench. Found a lump, taped over with cellotape. Ripped it off. Was an A4 envelope. I took a breath, preparing myself for what I'd find inside, and opened it.

The handwriting was fancy. Cursive. The type a girl unlike Trudie or I would write, paying painful attention to detail regardless of the reader. That didn't mean much. Necromancers had scribes. Either flesh puppets, or a literal hand sewn to an ear, writing whatever the necromancer dictated. Hands had muscle memory, and some bit of the soul still clung to the flesh, meaning that it wrote in the handwriting it had used while it had lived. Treth had told me once before about how necromancers on his world would hunt down scribes and poets just for their fancy handwriting. Pennames and anonymity were a matter of life and death there. Fortunately, I had not encountered the practice much during my forays into monster hunting. With recording devices and computers, necromancers didn't much need undead scribes. But some still must have used them. Perhaps for practice, perhaps for vanity, or perhaps just because they could.

The letter got straight to the point:

"Your friend is alive. For now. She is not in my custody, but I know who has her. As a part of the bargain, here is everything I know about her whereabouts.

You have encountered the tritely named *Blood Cartel* before. The mimic, you so luckily tracked and slew, was one of their assets. A trap meant to find hapless wanderers. The Cartel had trained the beast to camouflage itself, and then disciplined it into only eating very few victims, storing the others in a compartment in its stomach for retrieval.

As you may have guessed from the name, the Blood Cartel are a syndicate of higher vampires. Typical vampiric organised crime, but hyper-focused as of late. While other undead and vampire gangs fight among themselves, the Blood Cartel has united a few of those willing to take their affliction and profession seriously. For what exactly, I do not know. What I do know is that the Blood Cartel is behind the Eternity Lounge abductions. How do I know this? Well, I was the one who helped them. Was simple, really. A muscle freezing miasma. The vampires were more efficient in their retrieval of the human occupants than I previously thought they'd be. No time was wasted to lick the necks of young, succulent women. Like good little dockworkers, they moved all their prizes into a truck and drove off to an unknown location. I didn't even need to bring in my pets to help.

But: why am I telling you all this?

I owe no loyalty to the vampires. They are clients I can do without. But you, Kat. You're interesting. I'd rather watch your ascension as legendary freelancer than help some bloodsuckers get their next meal.

I look forward to further correspondence. And, perhaps, we can meet again and away from the cold air of North Road this time."

Chapter 17. Cartel

The cloaked figure. The North Road necromancer who'd strangled me with dark magic and led me to Jeremiah's lair. Was I playing into the necromancer's schemes when I killed Jeremiah? And was I further helping it by ignoring Conrad and going after these vampires?

"I don't like this," Treth said.

"Me neither. But, Trudie."

Treth nodded. He understood. We didn't have a lot in common, but we shared the same values. Friends meant something.

"So, vampires have Trudie…"

Saying it aloud sent a shiver up my spine. Blood suckers had my friend. Would she still even be alive?

Another shiver.

And if she was alive, would she be a ghoul or vampire? Would she be the Trudie I once knew? And if she wasn't, would I have the stomach to put her down?

As if he had read my mind, Treth said, "If she's turned, then it isn't her anymore. Even if she's a higher vampire. Even if she remembers you. It won't be her anymore. It'll be a monster…"

"And we slay monsters…"

I finished.

"Fuck," I swore aloud. I'd faced a lot of shit in my life, but never something like this. It was too much.

Vampires. I'd faced my fair share of lesser, but never higher. And never a gang of them. Didn't know the first thing about vampire organised crime besides that it existed. But I knew someone who might.

I dialled Miriam, damn the time. Luckily, the voice that answered didn't sound irritated, only curious.

"Ms Drummond? Sticking to business hours, I see."

"The Blood Cartel," I said, keeping my voice steady.

"Vampire syndicate. An uneasy alliance of a few of the top vampire gangs in Hope City. Interviewed a few of their low-rung members. What about them?"

"My friend has been taken by them. I need to get her back."

Silence. I heard an owl hoot somewhere off in the distance. An ominous sound. I couldn't help but look up at the crow. It was gone.

"Your friend may still be alive," Miriam said.

"How do you know?"

"The Blood Cartel isn't the usual vampire racket. I tried to contact their members to learn more about Robben Island and its rift-borne ruins. Under...duress, they revealed some things to me. The ruins on Robben Island are, as I hypothesised, of vampiric origin. And more than that, they didn't come to this world by accident. They were sent here – meant as an anchor point to our world."

She paused, and I replied. "What does this mean for Trudie?"

"Your friend is probably not being kept as food or as a thrall, but as a component for some primal vampiric ritual. And if my theory is correct, this ritual will be undertaken not this night but the next, during the full moon."

Some pre-Cataclysmic notions were more real than others. Full moons were, indeed, magical. Werewolves were triggered by them, weylines and sorcerers were strengthened, and many rituals had to be undertaken underneath their glow.

"Kat," Miriam said, using my first name for once. "Don't do anything rash. There is a reason even I haven't gone to Robben Island to conduct my research. It is a hotspot for rift surges and, if my field researchers are accurate, a prevalent hunting ground for lesser vampires."

"If my friend is there, I have no choice. And if the vampires are doing a ritual, should we really be letting them complete it?"

Miriam paused, considering.

"I would start in the morning. There is a bar called the Quantum in Old Town. Vampires use it during the day when they don't feel like sleeping. You can recognise Blood Cartel members by their tattoo. A red teardrop."

"Thanks, Miriam. I owe you one."

I was about to hang up when Miriam spoke. "If you do make your way to Robben Island, I want to hear what you found. That should be ample repayment."

"You'll be the first I tell. Good night."

"Good night, Miss Drummond, and good luck."

***

I returned the bicycle to the bench and walked the rest of the way home. It was 4am when I got there. I'd need to sleep, somehow, and then get to Old Town.

I turned into my street to the sight of Conrad's banged up Golf, and the man himself leaning up against the car with his arms crossed.

I bit my lip and steeled myself.

"Where the fuck have you been?!" Conrad shouted.

"Quiet. You'll wake the entire street."

"I don't care who wakes up!" he said, in a quieter voice, betraying his sentiments. "I called you a billion fucking times and you're out for an evening stroll. Do you know what you did? It wasn't just a fucking simple call out, Kat. Wasn't some zombie making noise in a well. It was a fucking zombie horde ripping up a speakeasy in the border slums. Fifteen people died before Puretide got off their arses and purged the place. Had to put down eight fucking more people who'd turned. What the fuck were you thinking?"

Conrad stopped his tirade but kept breathing heavily. Never thought I'd see him like this. He didn't look a bit like his normal used-car salesman self. He was dishevelled and dripping with sweat. I'd also never heard him swear so much in my life.

But that wasn't my biggest concern.

I'd let people die.

Was it worth it?

"The Eternity Lounge," I said. "I received a call from someone. A necromancer, I think. Told me what happened with the Eternity Lounge."

Conrad looked like he was about to yell, then he paused. Looked curious. I continued.

"The Lounge was raided by a vampire gang called the *Blood Cartel*. They're abducting people to be used in a ritual. The mimic was theirs, as well."

"The mimic? Vampires? Slow down, Kat…"

I didn't. "They're going to be doing something with the people they've been collecting during the full moon. My friend is among them. I'm sorry about what happened, but my friend comes first."

"And you got this information…"

"From a necromancer."

Conrad put both hands to his face and then dropped them, exasperated.

"I cross-checked the info with Miriam LeBlanc, Conrad. I'm not going loony. There's some big shit about to happen, and my friend is caught in the middle of it."

"I'm not one to trust necromancers, Kat. But if you spoke to Miriam and she thinks it could be true…"

He turned around, rubbed his hands together. It was chilly. Needed to be indoors. The sweat from my night exertions was amplifying the winter air on my body. I shook a little, from cold and the tail-end of my adrenaline.

"Shit, Kat. This is not in our paygrade," he finally said, stroking his hand across his dishevelled hair. "If the Council aren't paying, and a private client isn't either, then we aren't gonna get paid at all. And this sounds too hard for a pro-bono case."

"It isn't about money, Conrad. It's about my friend. If I need to go on *vacation* to save her, then so be it."

Conrad turned and looked me in the eyes. What was he looking for? My motivation? If I was testing him? I looked back. Held his gaze. Finally, he sighed.

"I'll help any way I can. Will first try to see if I can get a contract on the Cartel. If I can't, I'll unfortunately not be able to send any freelancers to help you."

I glared at him and he raised his palms up defensively. "I'm at the end of my last pay check, Kat. I can't afford to pay hunters when I'm not even eating properly."

I sighed. Couldn't blame him. I saw a freshly eaten can of beans in his car.

"Go to sleep, Kat," he said. "You look like shit and there's not much you can do if you're about to pass out. I'll phone around."

"Tight deadline."

"I know. But I'll do my best. Phone your Drakenbane friends in the morning. That Brett guy likes you."

"Likes to play games with me."

"Beggars can't be choosers."

I nodded. "Goodnight, Conrad."

He nodded back and got back into his car/home. I wondered why he didn't sleep in his office. Zoning laws, probably.

Duer and Alex were both asleep when I got home. I managed to make it to the couch when darkness took me. I couldn't remember my dreams when I woke up, but I knew they'd been the worst I'd had in ages.

Chapter 18.   Excessive Force

"Kat." I heard a disembodied voice mutter in the dark. I could hear it, but not exactly pinpoint its identity. It was the prototypical voice. A generic shard of communication, as if someone had sent me a printed note with a vague message. Was it the necromancer, disturbing me in my sleep as it did in life? There were plenty of dark magics that could be used to infest someone's dreams. Or was it Trudie, calling me across the black divide that now existed between us. Was she already dead, and was her spirit talking to me? Or was it just someone trying to wake me up...

"Kat," the voice repeated, gaining a sense of identity and emotion. I felt a hand on my shoulder but didn't see it. My head felt like it was in a vice grip. I hadn't gotten enough sleep, and now I was being ripped away from it. I hoped adrenaline would be enough to stop a splitting headache.

"Kat," the voice said again, anxiously. I wrenched my eyes open and saw Pranish looming over me, his hands on my shoulders. Duer was floating next to him, looking curious and concerned. His glow was throbbing frenetically, a sign that he was also anxious.

"Pranish? How'd you get in?"

"I've got a spare key," he said, taking it out of his pocket to prove the point. I'd forgotten I had given one to him as well as Trudie. My apartment was kinda a common room for them. I often needed them to be able to access the room when I was on long hunts, or when I was too comatose to open the room myself when they'd gotten me out of a bind.

"You weren't answering your phone," Pranish said. I sat up and rubbed my eyes and head. I felt like the way Conrad said I looked. Shit. I glanced at the time on my cell phone. 8am. I also had five missed calls from Pranish and a text from Conrad. I opened it:

"Council stonewalling me. Threatening to take me off the roster if I press any further. Sorry, Kat! Best I could do. Good luck!"

I couldn't be angry at Conrad. He'd tried his best. I felt a growing warmth for him just because he'd tried. The Council, on the other hand...

What game were those parasites playing? Was breaking up vampire organised crime too legitimate of a job for them to sanction? Would a buck going towards eliminating a human trafficking ring be too much money not going towards exterminating griffons and drakes?

Fucking typical. Council didn't do its job in the slums and didn't do its job in the city. It was a miracle it even kept the Titan Mages funded and Adamastor asleep.

"We're on our own," I said, gloomily.

"For what?"

I hadn't told him the news from last night!

"Vampires have her, Pranish. Fucking vamp cartel. Gonna sacrifice her tonight for some cultist shit."

Pranish covered his mouth and paled. I continued.

"Conrad tried to see if he could help, but Council doesn't give a flying fuck about it, as usual."

"What if...what if we ask Andy?"

Andy. I hadn't thought about him. Since his oddball behaviour at the Eternity Lounge, I'd felt a bit offish with him. But he was still my friend, and Trudie's. And his dad was a Councillor. He had pulled strings to get me into the Club. He could help me with this. Could get the Council to put a full bounty on the Blood Cartel. Could have Puretide and Drakenbane jostling to collect some vamp heads. Trudie'd be saved in hours, if not minutes!

I dialled Andy. He picked up after two rings.

"Hey, Kat."

I didn't respond immediately. He sounded different. Not as confident as he usually was. Hesitant. Tired. Was he also looking into Trudie's disappearance? I felt a bit of warmth reignite for him.

"Andy, I know what happened to Trudie. She was taken by vampires. Tried to get Conrad to get the Council to put a bounty on them, but they're stone-walling him."

No response.

"Andy?"

"Um, yeah. Shit, Kat. How do you know all this?"

He sounded odd. Very odd. As if he had a massive hangover and was looking for an excuse to hang up.

I tried to cool myself, but my voice still came out as a scolding hiss. "I spent all day and all night looking into it, that's how. You pulled strings at the Eternity Lounge. Please do it again. Trudie's life may depend on it."

A pause. A long pause. I was about to repeat myself when he finally answered.

"I'm sorry, Kat. I can't."

I was about to say, "Why the fuck not?"

But instead said, "Can you at least come back us up? If we can't get the agencies on this, we'll need to do it ourselves. We have until tonight to save her."

"I'm sorry. But I can't."

I did say it then. "Why the fuck not?"

He replied in his same tired tone. "It's...personal. I'm sorry, Kat. I really am. I can't do anything today."

"You'll leave Trudie to die?" I couldn't help but yell.

No reply. I heard him breathing, slowly.

I hung up.

I was fuming. What the fuck was more important than saving my friend? His friend! A person's life was on the line and he was more concerned with personal petty bullshit?

Pranish moved and my head swivelled to him. I must have looked as angry as I felt, as he flinched.

"Andy is refusing to help."

Pranish's expression darkened.

"We don't have to do it alone, though," I said, dialling Brett. "I've got hunters who might be able to help."

"Katty!" Brett answered, and I immediately regretted my decision. Brett was a decent hunter, but he loved to tease. "Phoning outside of business hours. This mean you want to go out for coffee?"

"My friend has been abducted by a vampire cartel. I need help to save her before the full moon tonight."

A pause.

"Guy and I will be at your place asap."

He hung up before I could thank him.

Brett was irritating. He was arrogant. He was cock-sure to the point of juvenility. But he got things done. He'd helped me before. Saved me before. Maybe I should actually start being a bit nicer to him. He was a good person.

"Hey, Katty," he said as he arrived in his black jeep blaring power metal, Guy checking his dual machine pistols in the passenger seat. I couldn't help but roll my eyes. I wanted to be nice, but not until he cut this "Katty" crap.

Guy got out of the passenger seat and offered it to me. Pranish approached the vehicle.

"I'm coming too. I've been stocking up on combat spells for weeks."

I raised my eyebrow quizzically at that. "Why?"

Pranish shrugged. "Why not?"

"I'd never say no to backup. Especially against vamps. We don't have Cindy or some Puretide light mage with us, so a wizard will be welcome," Brett said.

I nodded. I was a bit apprehensive about Pranish coming along, didn't want to lose another friend, but wasn't my right to stop him. Trudie was his friend too.

We all entered the car and Brett turned down the stereo. It was playing *Through the Fire and Flames* by Dragonforce. Definitely a song to get one amped. Rumour had it that it was the song Thor listened to when he banished Fafnir from Berlin.

"So, where are we headed?"

"Vamp expert said we could find a Blood Cartel member at a bar in Old Town. Quantum."

Guy shifted in his seat. Brett and I turned to face him.

"Vamp bar. Lost a bounty in it last year. Two-bit scumbag vamp who was selling bites to stupid teens," he said. "Problem is that the bar is private property. Without a warrant, which I didn't get back then, we aren't allowed to enter it without permission."

"Then we storm the place," Brett said. I didn't hide my surprise and looked at the man and his square, stubbled jaw. He was serious.

Guy didn't look keen on that idea. I often got the impression that he was the more reasonable of the pair. They were not only partners at Drakenbane, but roommates. At least they complemented each other well.

"Let's go and discuss the plan on the way," Brett said, putting the address to the bar into his GPS and pulling off.

"We could go in and act like customers," Pranish offered.

Guy shook his head. "Won't work. The owner only lets in vamps."

"Aren't vamps a prohibited species?" I asked.

Guy frowned. "Grey area. They aren't *persona non grata*. Technically, they fall under the Spirit of the Law's protection. But because there's almost never an innocent vampire, their rights kinda fall away. But it is innocent till proven guilty. The Quantum proprietor is very good at keeping the Council out of his business."

On the drive to Old Town, we discussed other plans. Catching customers before they entered was ruled out cause the vamps typically came in through underground entrances. We didn't know where any of these vamp tunnels came up, so couldn't wait inside them. Guy asked why we didn't ask the Council for a bounty on the Cartel. I explained that the Council were morons.

By the time we reached the concrete jungle of Old Town, we had decided that, illegal or not, the only way was to storm the place. When we came to that decision, an uncomfortable silence fell on the car. But neither Brett nor Guy turned back or uttered their disapproval. They were about to commit a crime for me. Sure, it was killing vamps, but they could get expelled from Drakenbane and arrested if they were caught. And I wasn't offering anything in the way of pay. So, why? Why help?

I looked at Brett as he drove, eyes on the road. He wasn't smiling. The only sign of his usual self was his tapping his fingers on the steering wheel in time with the beat of the song.

"Because it is the right thing to do," Treth offered, guessing what I was thinking. I looked out the window.

The right thing to do.

Maybe. Maybe that's all that it needed to be.

Quantum was so nondescript that if we didn't have the GPS, we wouldn't have found it. It was located in the night club district but had none of the neon signs and flashy branding like its neighbours. It was just a metal door in a mass-constructed row of grey brick commercial real estate. There was a closed iron peephole in the door. I doubted a vamp would open it at this time of day. Clubs didn't typically stay open during the day, so nobody would find it suspicious if a knock at the door went unanswered.

"Park in that alley," I said to Brett, who did so.

The car went quiet. Brett had long since turned off his music.

"Plan of attack," Brett said, his face not giving away any emotion. It was the expression he had during the attack at UCT. Business-Brett. "We need to break down that door. We can try kick it, or shotgun it, but if it is barred, that won't be enough."

"I've got a lockpicking scroll with me," Pranish said.

"Always good to have a wizard," Brett nodded. "But won't help if it is barred."

"Detonation scroll."

Brett raised his eyebrow. "What were you planning? Domestic terrorism?"

Pranish shrugged and gave a faint smile, the first since Trudie's abduction. "Hey, gotta practice for any line of work. Economy is tough."

Brett grinned. I got the feeling he liked Pranish. Respected him. Maybe I should do the same. Hell, if these scrolls work, I'll be the first to sign up to Pranish's fan club.

"I say we go in guns blazing. We've got silver shot, so they'll go down eventually," Guy said. "Vamps have good perception. No use sneaking in. Detonation scroll first. Boom, and then Brett goes in. I'll follow. We eliminate the biggest threats and then…what then?"

"We need a member alive. Any vamp with a blood teardrop tattoo."

"Vain bastards. Makes them easy to catch," Brett added. His expression was still business-like, despite the jest.

"How will we make him talk?" Guy asked.

"I've got some ideas."

My voice had taken on an ice-cold tone that brought silence to the car. Finally, Brett broke the silence.

"No use waiting. We're on a tight timer here. Ticks will be here mere hours after we break in." He grinned at the jab at our less than stellar city law enforcement.

"Private security is a different matter," he added. So, in and out. I'm not scared of ticks, but I'd rather not go to a disciplinary hearing before Drakenbane."

We exited the jeep. Guy and Brett retrieved their weapons from the trunk.

"Here," Guy said, tossing a padded black vest and white face-mask to Pranish, who hastily put them on. It was a bit too big for him. Guy and Brett's arms were easily double the size of Pranish's. Same went for their pecs.

"Want a weapon?" Guy added. Pranish shook his head and patted his satchel, multiple scrolls peeking out of it.

"Stay in the back," Guy said. "Out of trouble and flinging spells. How's the weyline here?"

Pranish closed his eyes for a second and then opened them. "Passable. Got some totems just in case we run dry."

Totems stored the energy of weylines for particular spells, allowing their usage away from the magical circuits. Sorcerers hated them. If given enough prep-time and money to buy the precious metals needed for their creation, a wizard could pretend to be a sorcerer far away from any weylines.

"No cameras," Brett said. He had been peeking around the corner of the alley. "No civvies. A good time. Let's go."

He put on a balaclava that made him look particularly criminal like and signed for us to follow him. I put on my black and white face-mask and followed.

The streets were empty. It was the clubbing district after all. Not much reason to be out here during the day. We did hear traffic, though. Lots of hooting. Couldn't forget that we were still in a major city. A boom was going to draw attention. Not to mention the subsequent gunshots. I frowned as I looked at Brett and Guy's guns. I'd seen guns fired before but had never been shot at. This was going to be a new experience. Hopefully, Brett and Guy were better shots than the vamps.

Brett and Guy flanked the door, guns drawn. I stood behind them and drew my swords. Pranish sifted through his satchel for the scroll. I hoped his combat scrolls were more easily accessible. Timing was everything in a fight. He wore a white hockey mask, I noticed. Made him look like an Indian Jason Voorhees.

Finally, Pranish found the right scroll. He took out some tack and stuck the scroll to the door, over the lock. I hoped he had it facing the right way. He said some gibberish words and then backed out of the way.

Nothing.

Then...

Boom.

The door fell off its hinges. Brett didn't skip a beat and charged right through. A shotgun blast sent ringing through my ears. Should've worn earplugs. Well, went to the healing mage every other day. May as well get my impending tinnitus cured while I'm there. Guy followed. I waited a second and charged right through after them.

The Quantum was a dark, seedy place. The type of place you'd imagine low-life vampire gangsters hanging out. I couldn't blame them for all the dirt, though. Especially the gun smoke, shotgun shells on the floor, shattered glass (collateral damage) and blood all over the concrete floor (intentional damage).

There were about five vamps inside. One dead. The one behind the bar looked pretty human, if not for his bared fangs. His arm was swiss-cheesed by shotgun pellets and he was trying to fire a pistol with his non-dominant hand. His shots were going wide, and Guy planted him with a quick burst of his machine pistol. A puff of pink mist, and the vamp fell. He'd be up soon enough if he wasn't beheaded or burnt.

I had never been in a firefight before. My prey usually didn't use guns. Some necromancers developed abhorrent and flesh puppets who maintained the muscle memory to use firearms, but they were rare. And while my prey was usually instinctively cunning, they were never intelligent. These vampires were different. They had thoughts in their blood-red eyes, sneers of conscious anger and guns in their hands. They reminded me a bit of Jeremiah Cox, and his abhorrent with angry eyes. I didn't shiver at the unpleasant thought. My mind was racing too fast for that. My heart felt like it was going to beat out of my chest. My head rang and my ears hurt. The gunshots in this enclosed space weren't helping. I smelled the acridity of gunpowder and the sting of liquor spilt out of now shattered bottles. I tasted blood. I had bitten my own tongue.

I wasn't scared, exactly. My heart beat too fast and I was too confused to be scared. I only saw flashes of images. Brett moving forward, firing his shotgun and pumping out a used shell after every bang. Guy dove behind a round aluminium topped table and turned it over, using it as some make-shift cover. Guy stood and lay down some fire with his dual machine-pistols. Brett pushed forward and took cover behind a booth. I was still behind a wall at the entrance, meant to keep out direct sunlight. I tried to advance, but a bullet chipped at the concrete and I felt the concrete shards pelt my pants. I froze. Pranish was frozen next to me.

And I realised that while I had seen so much horror, there were different types of things to fear. And this was one of them. So, I stayed frozen behind this flimsy concrete wall, deafened and white as a sheet.

You should know me by now. I like to get things done. I like to work alone because I want to be the hero. Maybe it's narcissism. Maybe it's just a plain old heroes complex. Treth has it too, so I can't be blamed completely. Regardless of what it is, I've got this intense need to be the one putting myself in harm's way.

But this was different. This wasn't a monster hunt. It wasn't anything I could participate in.

I looked at my impotent swords. They were so reliable. So sharp. They'd saved my life and made me so much money. But how could they compare to bullets?

I leaned around the corner. Guy and Brett were pinned. The vamps were unloading everything they had at them. Only the reinforced tables, probably meant to be protecting the vampire proprietor himself, were keeping my comrades alive. But for how long? And how long until reinforcements for the vamps came?

I looked at my swords again. My pitiful blades. Over the din of gunfire, I heard muttering. It was high pitched, anxious and speedy. Pranish had a scroll open, and he was reading as fast as he could, his shaking hands and the scroll were glowing. I knew he was crying underneath that mask. I was too. This wasn't our domain. We were kids. Just kids.

But kid or not, Pranish was doing something. And that is all I needed to spring into action.

I took a deep breath, and ran, keeping my head low and my swords to my sides. I felt a warmth touch me as Pranish threw a shield spell over me. I fell as a bullet grazed me. Only grazed. I hit the side of the bar counter with an oomph and checked myself for the wound. Nothing. I had been hit, but the shield had deflected it. Still hurt like I'd been pelted by a golf ball, though. Could deflect the round, but magic couldn't disobey physics. That force had to go somewhere. In this case, it went into the aether and my thigh. I felt it and it stung a little. Not too much. Would be a big black bruise in the end though. That's if we survived this.

"Dive forward," Treth said.

I did so immediately, rolling forward. My swords clanked on the ground. I heard the shotgun blast a moment afterwards. I'd thank Treth, but he'd saved my life so often like this that the thanks got a bit cheap.

The vampire barman stood behind the counter with a double-barrelled shotgun. He had pale, bordering white, skin and crimson eyes. He was far gone. A lot of vampires looked human, except for the fangs, but the longer they were afflicted, the more they started to morph. While their appearance also changed, so did their abilities. The barman's sleeves where he'd been shot were stained red. I saw one of the pellets push itself out of the vamp's flesh, the skin then smoothing over. He had two 9mm round sized scars on his forehead. Should've brought some silver. The purified metal didn't kill vampires outright but couldn't be healed as quickly.

I didn't need silver to kill a vampire though. Cause it didn't matter that the pellets were pushed out and that the two 9mm shells in his head only left a nasty scar that would heal itself if given time. It still bled. And if it could bleed, I could kill it.

I twisted my body into a sprinter's crouch, aimed at the barman who reached for his apron pockets for more shells. I didn't give him a chance. I pounced, swords before me, and pierced his skull with both. His mouth made an oh even as he continued fidgeting with his shotgun. Using the swords and his head, I lifted myself onto the counter and from my crouch, kicked him onto the ground behind the bar. Followed him, unsheathed my swords from his face and like a golfer, chopped his windpipe off with one stroke, and then another to lop off the rest of his head. His expression still shifted for seconds after he was beheaded.

They may be able to talk. They may be able to act the part. But vampires weren't human. They're monsters. I slay monsters.

The bar had a long mirror behind it. While humans used mirrors to spot vampire, vampires probably used mirrors to spot the human. Was pretty good surveillance. A human intruder would stand out in any crowd. In the mirror, they'd be all alone. I saw Brett and Guy's reflections pressing forward, and Pranish behind them, holding up a wall of light. I didn't see the vamps, but I saw puffs of fire and smoke.

"Don't forget why we're here," Treth said.

Why we're here? In the tableau, I almost had. This was not an extermination. We were looking for someone to interrogate.

"Can you see anyone?" I asked, hoping he could hear me over the cacophony. Treth didn't exactly see what I saw. He could swivel his vision around me, as if he was tethered to me.

A pause. I feared he couldn't hear me, but he replied.

"Man with the woollen hat. Red tear tattoo. Has one of those smaller guns but not firing. Looks angry."

Well, of course he's angry! He's a vampire, and we're invading his leisure time. He probably had a busy night of murder and abductions last night.

I made my way to the end of the bar, closest to the back, and risked peaking. As Treth had said, a vampire with a blood-red tattoo was fidgeting with a pistol. Probably jammed.

Two bangs. One of the other vamps fell. He still squirmed, but Brett used the opportunity to advance, firing as he went. The vamp with the jammed pistol looked up and I saw fear in his eyes. A very human fear. He wasn't that far gone. Looked human. He turned and pushed through a backdoor, disappearing.

Guy had said that the vampires used a network of tunnels to get in here. If he got lost in there, we'd never find him. I couldn't give up this chance. He could be the only thing that could lead me to Trudie.

I leapt over the bar counter, feeling shattered glass crunch into my gloves. I kicked off and followed through the back door before any of the surviving vamps could spot me.

The backroom of the Quantum was even darker than the front. There was only a dim light, illuminating the bathroom door and a series of metal shelves filled with unlabelled bottles. I thought they'd keep the blood refrigerated. May be something else, though.

No sign of any place the vamp could hide in here. I moved to the bathroom, kicking it open. The bathroom was oddly clean. Vampires weren't undead but had some similarities. For instance, they didn't need to use the bathroom. There were three stalls, all with closed doors. I went to the first and kicked it open. Nothing but a spotless porcelain toilet. I winced at the noise I had made. But a vamp could hear me regardless. So, could be loud.

I kicked the next door and was rewarded by the sight of a toilet lifted up above the ground on hidden hinges, with a ladder below. Bingo.

I sheathed my swords and drew my seax. The larger blades would be too hard to climb with. But I still needed a weapon at the ready. I dropped down and descended into the dark.

Dim lights lined the wall every ten or so metres. Vampires did have good dark vision, but younger vampires still needed some light source to see. Their older kin didn't need any light at all. They could feel their surroundings and know exactly where to pounce on their next meal.

The vamp hadn't gotten far. He was panting, doubled over. He was definitely new. Still very human. I frowned.

"He isn't human," Treth said.

But he used to be.

But so were zombies.

I drew my swords. The almost inaudible tinkle of the blades leaving their scabbards alerted the vamp and he went off running again. I gritted my teeth and gave chase.

What was I doing? I needed him alive. How did you catch a vampire alive?

And then I recalled the bullets pushing out of the barman's head.

It'd be easy to take him alive. Just had to make sure I didn't burn him or cut off his head. No risk of that.

My feet beat down on the concrete and so did his. A true higher vamp would outpace me any day, but he wasn't a true higher vamp yet.

I brought my sword back, preparing to thrust as I ran. I gained on him and his dark back grew closer and closer and then...

We both tumbled with an oomph as I felt my blade enter into his back, puncturing a lung. He cried out in pain and collapsed, me on top of him. I ripped off his woollen beanie and grabbed him by the hair. With my grip on his recently shampooed black locks, I rammed his face into the concrete below. Again, and again, and again. He stopped squirming but was still breathing. Vampires were pretty resilient. Made my job easier. I didn't have to hold back.

I stood, my foot still keeping him prone, drew my other sword and slashed at his ankles. He screamed, and I couldn't help but wince. It was a human scream. But he wasn't human. A human would be dead by now. Yet, he still felt pain. A lot of it.

I bit my lip and thought of Trudie. My next stab was right in his brain.

He went lights out.

Chapter 19.   Sunlight

The vampire blinked twice. He first noticed that the pain had stopped. Then he noticed that his hands and legs were bound. Finally, he noticed the group of masked figures surrounding him.

"Finally awake?" I asked him. It was the first time I had ever spoken to a vampire. He was young. Mid twenties. Had the stubble you get when you can't grow it any longer. His skin was not as pale as the barman's but was getting there. We'd confirmed that he was indeed a vampire after the others caught up with me. The fangs were hard to hide. We then put him in a series of trash-bags and carried him out to the car. A few passers-by ran from the masked crew, but there weren't any cops.

We took the vamp to an abandoned apartment block in one of those middling suburbs inbetween the Southern Suburbs and Old Town. Luckily, the elevator still worked, and we took the still comatose vamp up to the top storey, closed all the blinds and then strapped him to a chair. The whole ordeal had cost us time. It was midday now. Only hours till Trudie's death.

The vamp didn't respond immediately to my question, so I poked him with the tip of my sword. Drew blood. I kept my face steely, but I did feel an instinctual guilt from the act. He looked human. He was intelligent. It wasn't the same as cutting up zombies. But he was a monster. His under-eye tattoo made him one, even if his vampirism did not.

"You are a member of the Blood Cartel," I said. I must have surprised him, as he looked me in the eyes. I wasn't afraid of any sort of hypnotism. He wasn't a true vampire. Only they had mind powers.

He didn't respond, but his actions were good enough for me to proceed.

"Your gang has a friend of mine, and a lot of innocent people. Tell me where they're being held, and I'll let you go free."

He sneered, and I caught a glimpse of his fang.

"I don't know what you're talking about."

"Cut the shit, vamp! Your necromancer ally snitched. I know all about the sacrifices and the human trafficking."

I stabbed him in the leg with my dusack. He winced and bit his lip, drawing blood. I surprised even myself.

"If you want to go free, tell us where the prisoners are!"

Silence. He opened his eyes. I looked into them and saw anger. Understandable. He spat on my mask.

I wriggled my dusack a bit, being rewarded with his pained squirming. I withdrew it. He looked relieved. That was the problem. Pain was finite. He knew he'd heal. No scars. No lasting damage. Couldn't even pull out his fangs. They'd grow back. You had to give vampires silver caps or braces to stop their teeth from re-growing. Regeneration was a bitch to deal with. Pain was one thing, but without the fear of lasting damage and death, it was just a temporary inconvenience.

"Want me to rough him up?" Brett offered. I wasn't sure what he could do worse than what I'd done to the vamp already.

"No, I've got a better idea."

I made my way to the blinds and checked the time. If I was correct, the sun was shifting westward. It was just overhead right now. This was a west-facing window. The sun would slowly start to seep in if the blinds were opened.

The vampire was thinking the same thing as me. It was subtle, but I saw real fear in his eyes. His pupils dilated, and he poked his inner cheek with his tongue.

"If you told us where the prisoners are headed," I said, playing with the strings of the blinds. "You would probably be killed. Head chopped off. Quick. Painless. That's if they found out, of course. No guarantee of that. A lot of vamps died at the Quantum. One missing won't be that suspicious. Could easily get away from the Cartel. Could head to the Zulu Empire, or up north. I hear ogres are terrified of vampires. Could start your own gang with them. Could even take a ship. Not many sirens this time of year and I don't think they have much of an effect on vamps."

I paused and clutched the string of the blinds with a taut fist.

"That's if you told us. If you don't? Well, I hear death by sunlight is very painful for a vampire."

I didn't know that at all but was safe to assume that it was at least partly true. The vampire bound to a metal chair seemed to agree.

"Vampirism is a great boon, right?" I continued. "That's what you probably thought when you got bit.

266

Super strength, immortality, regeneration, and can even create your own army of thralls. But it comes with a brutal side effect."

I opened a slit in the blinds with a flick, letting in a sliver of light that touched the dirty wooden floor just in front of the vampire's toes. He looked at the streak of golden light as if he was looking down the barrel of a gun.

"Let's start again," I said, hand still on the blinds string. "How about your name?"

No reply. I made a motion to tug on the blinds.

"Henrik," he said, his voice cracking. "Henrik Calvi."

"So, Henrik Calvi, how loyal to the Blood Cartel are you?"

No reply, but I saw his lips move. Just needed a bit more coaxing.

"Bring Henrik closer to the window, please," I said, indicating Brett. I felt like a super villain giving the order.

"I'm glad you're on my side," Treth said, trying to jest. I didn't find it very funny.

Brett put his hands on the back of Henrik's chair, who immediately twitched and spoke.

"They'll kill me regardless," he said, fear in his voice. "They know everything about vamps in the city. Won't be able to get out."

He shook his head and continued.

"Ain't gonna talk. Better burn me."

Brett looked at me. I nodded. He shifted the chair closer. It scraped across the ground and Henrik shook violently. The sunlight was on his shoes.

"I'll ask again, Henrik. Where is the Cartel keeping their prisoners?"

He shook his head, reluctantly.

I opened the blinds halfway. The sunlight drifted all the way up to his chest. He was lucky he was clothed everywhere but his head. The warmth must have gotten to him, though, as he screamed.

"If you want this to stop, then tell us what we want to know, Henrik!" I shouted over his cries.

His screams were incomprehensible. Garbled by fear. But he wasn't cracking. Not yet.

"It seems you need a taste of vitamin D."

I looked at Brett. "Take off his shoes."

Brett didn't hesitate. He leant down and started taking off the vampire's black leather loafers. Designer, if I might add. The vampire kept shouting in fear, but as his shoe came off, he screamed in genuine agony.

I could hear the sizzle. Smoke rose from his foot and I smelt burning flesh. If I wasn't so jacked up on adrenaline, I'd have wanted to vomit. I saw Pranish leave the room. Didn't blame him.

I closed the blinds. I could still smell the burnt flesh, but the sizzling stopped. I went up to Henrik and clutched him by the jaw. He stopped screaming. I saw tears in his eyes.

He's not human, I reminded myself. *He's a monster.*

"Henrik," I said calmly when I wanted to yell and cry. "Tell us where they're being kept, or your chest will be next."

A pause, and then Henrik looked down. I let go of his jaw and stepped back, arms on my hips.

"They're being kept at a warehouse by the wharfs at Atlantic Beach. 11B-A. They're being shipped to Robben Island tonight by speedboat."

"Thank you," I said, sincerely, but maintaining a voice of angry disdain.

"We better bring the vamp with," Guy said. "To make sure he isn't lying."

"He's a liability," Brett replied. "I say let him burn here."

Henrik looked up at him with abject horror, and then at me.

"You said I could go free!"

"Can't let him go warn the Cartel," Brett said.

"But he could be lying," Guy added.

"I did as you asked! I promise it's true. Honest!" Henrik sobbed.

"The vampire will come with us," I finally said. "Get him something so he won't char."

Guy nodded. "I'll go get something."

Brett nodded as well, accepting the decision.

"They'll kill me," Henrik said.

"Not if we kill them first," I replied, and left the room.

There was a small bathroom down the hall from the abandoned flat and I rushed to it once nobody could see me. I heard Pranish retching in one of the apartment's bathrooms. I went in the opposite direction, rushed into a bathroom and closed the door.

"You did well," Treth said.

I took off my mask and looked at myself in the bathroom mirror. Sweat caked wisps of my hair to my forehead. My eyes were puffy. The ever-present bags under my eyes looked even more pronounced by the layers of perspiration on my face. I was panting. Enough panting for all the exertions of the day so far. Could I handle more? This wasn't even the battle. It was prep-work. If I was flagging now, could I handle what was to come?

And would my conscience allow it?

"Fuck, Kat," I said to myself. "They're just fucking vampires."

Treth gave his wordless agreement. He agreed with my spoken sentiments. But the words didn't help. Henrik's face was burnt into my mind. Pale, but human. His pain was human, and I had caused it.

"Have some water," Treth said.

With a shaking hand, I turned the tap. The flat still had running water. I wondered why nobody was living here. Probably a mistake with the Council. They sometimes forgot to turn off the power and water to abandoned buildings. I sipped the water, but it tasted acrid. Nothing could have tasted good at the moment.

I forced myself to drink more, and when I finally had enough, I turned off the tap.

"You can do this, Kat," Treth said. "You've gone through worse for lesser reasons. This matters more than anything we've ever done before. You'll find the strength."

I nodded and left the bathroom.

I smelled tobacco smoke as I exited. Brett was leaning up against the wall a few metres away, taking a long drag on a cigarette. His balaclava was off, and his dark hair stuck to his head like it was caked with glue. I walked to him and he offered me a cigarette from the box. I declined and leant up against the wall next to him.

I normally hated the smell of cigarettes, but Brett was smoking the same brand as Trudie.

"Why are you helping me?" I finally asked.

Brett took another drag, blew a cloud of smoke, and answered. "Because it is the right thing to do."

That answer shocked both me and Treth. I looked at Brett, the Drakenbane agent who always called me Katty and kept me up late on hunts. Had I really had him all wrong?

He turned to me and grinned. "And cause it might win me a date."

I shoved him, and he laughed. Some silence.

Finally, I asked. "Can you teach me how to shoot?"

"You did fine at the bar, Kat. Killed an armed higher vamp and incapacitated another."

I shook my head. "Could have done more. I love these blades, but they're just blades. This is the 21st century. Cataclysm or not, guns still reign. I don't want to go blank in a firefight again. I don't want to cower at the back while others go ahead. I want to learn how to shoot and then get a gun."

I felt a hint of disapproval from Treth. I got the feeling he didn't like guns. Didn't like a lot of the things from Earth. I ignored him.

Brett took a puff and looked into the aether, contemplating.

"There's a range near Glencairn. Empty during the week. Can train you there."

I nodded, sternly. "Thanks. We can go there after this is all done. If we survive."

Brett looked at me with another grin. "So, it's a date?"

I rolled my eyes and left him hanging. I walked to the room containing Henrik and entered. Guy was putting a hoodie over his head, with a balaclava and sunglasses to boot. Pranish had recovered and was watching intently. He smelled like puke and sweat. I walked up to him and gave him a nod. He nodded back. He knew the unspoken message.

We were going to save Trudie.

Chapter 20.   Deadline

Cloud cover darkened the afternoon sky and Hope City traffic slowed us down by hours. It was 6pm when we arrived at Atlantic Beach. I couldn't help but feel a bit apprehensive driving into the neighbourhood. It was uncomfortably close to North Road, and where I had met the necromancer who had put me down this path. Brett and Guy had already phoned in to Drakenbane to call in sick. They had never missed a day of work before this, so they had plenty of sick days left to squander. But, I still wondered why they were doing this for me. Sick day or not, they only got paid when they got a bounty. They weren't rich. Didn't have excess capital to fall on. They were like me. Living hunt to hunt. But they had taken a day off work to risk their lives, to save my friend. All because it was the right thing to do.

Henrik had a bag over his head and was being kept tied up at Pranish and Guy's feet. We didn't want him to see our faces and we couldn't risk driving around busy Old Town with our masks on. Cops were pretty lax, but four people in a jeep wearing masks and balaclavas would warrant a stop and search. Usually, monster hunters could get away with a lot. Not just anyone can walk around a mall carrying swords and wearing combat armour. You needed the permission of an agency or a freelancer card. Before Conrad, I didn't have such a card and needed to keep my behaviour appropriate to that of a civilian 19-year-old girl. Conrad's monster hunter ID that he had given me had definitely liberated me and made my life easier.

"Sun's down," Guy said. "Masks on and the vamp can get some fresh air."

Guy never called Henrik by his name. I got the impression that he really hated vampires – saw them the same way I saw zombies. It wasn't the sort of dislike you have for monsters in general. Sure, I could easily kill a ghoul, but I didn't despise them exactly. Undead were a different story. I really hated them. So much so that I didn't need to be paid to kill them. Maybe that's why Guy was doing this? Maybe, hurting vampires was all the incentive he needed. A small part of me, the Treth part, hoped I was wrong. Hate wasn't a good motivator. Treth had convinced me of that.

Still, Guy very coolly pulled Henrik onto the seat, in between himself and Pranish, and took off his black sack.

Our masks were all back on as we didn't need to worry about people finding our posse suspicious. The sun was setting fast and the streets were relatively empty as we turned up into the warehouse lots of Atlantic beach.

"Where to from here, vamp?" Brett asked, echoing Guy's behaviour. I didn't think it was from a personal distaste, though. More copying his friend. Could have been wrong, though. Guy and Brett were like me and most other monster hunters. We didn't see vampires as human or human-like. That's what let you kill them. You had to have a modicum of disrespect for life to thrive in this line of work. You seldom found vegetarian monster hunters.

"It's at the end, past that fence. Going to have to go out on foot."

"Lucky the sun is down," Brett said.

"Yes, I am lucky," Henrik snarled.

I frowned. I didn't like it. Fighting vampires during the day was hard enough. Fighting them at night? I just had to hope that these vampires were too busy working to notice us. And if they did notice us, that we'd somehow manage to break through.

Above all, I really hoped we wouldn't run into a true vampire. With just the four of us, I don't think we'd survive.

"Henrik," I said. I preferred calling him by his name. Didn't mean I was humanising him. I just felt using someone's name made one more persuasive. "Tell us about the guards."

He shrugged. "Not much. Didn't think we'd be found. Ticks are lax."

Right ironic that he was calling police ticks when he was a vampire. Interesting about the lack of guards though. Would the Blood Cartel really be relying on secrecy alone? I doubted it. The Quantum had been armed to the hilt and it was just a bar. This place was going to be crawling with vampires.

"Any true vampires?" I asked.

He peered at me with his reddening eyes. He looked surprised at the question. And then, deeply uncertain.

"No." It didn't sound like a lie. But he didn't sound certain, either. Was he not sure?

"Perhaps he means to reinforce his earlier lie," Treth suggested. It was uncanny how it seemed he could almost ready my mind. "The idea of a true vampire to him must be so absurd that by admitting that there is none here, he thinks we will believe that there are no guards."

Treth had a point. Never lie completely. Always give a little bit of truth. But there seemed to be more to the story. Henrik wasn't lying, but that was because he was ignorant as to whether there really was a true vampire among their ranks. That made things a tad scarier.

Brett stopped the car and turned off the engine. We got out and stretched our legs. It had been a long drive. The traffic had been so bad that Pranish was even able to get out of the car, buy some burgers, and get back in before we'd moved much at all. Too bad it was too far to walk, and he had to keep this damn vamp to ensure we got the right place.

"We taking him with?" I asked, indicating Henrik, who looked like a dejected cat.

"Have to," Guy said. "Don't want a vamp at our backs."

I bit my lip. Didn't seem like a good idea. Guy noticed.

"Not much choice. But it'll behave. Otherwise it's getting beheaded."

I was the only one with a blade big enough for beheadings. Seems Guy was placing the responsibility firmly on me if something went wrong. Great.

We checked our equipment, Henrik still in the car with his arms bound behind his back and a balaclava covering his mouth and features. Satisfied, we let him out.

"Lead the way," Brett said, and Henrik proceeded. We followed, weapons drawn. Tense. A feeling we had all had before – some more than others. That time before a hunt. That time before you leap upon the target. That time as you watch if the zombie takes the bait, or if hours of prep work would be for nothing. But this time it was tenser. This time, it mattered more than all the others.

I'm coming, Trudie. I just hoped she'd be alive when I got there.

The cold, salty air was unpleasantly chilly where it managed to get through the cracks of my getup. My mind unduly focused on the spikes of ice invading the back of my neck, a slit underneath my t-shirt and by my ankles. It was a defence mechanism of the brain that it focused on the mundane, so one didn't destroy oneself fearing the ginormous.

There were a lot of warehouses on the lot and it was probably a good thing that we had Henrik. None of the warehouses were clearly marked. The vampire seemed resigned to his fate and walked unemotionally forward. I was directly behind him, flanked by Brett and Guy. Pranish took up the rear.

This wasn't my friend's domain, and while he had been performing more than adequately, I feared for his psyche. He wouldn't sleep for days. He'd never rest easy again.

We were nearing the end of the lot and I could see glimpses of the tumultuous coastline in between the concrete and metal-clad warehouses. I felt a drip on my shoulder. It was starting to rain.

And then, Henrik shouted. Incomprehensible, as my blade found its mark and his head cleanly left his body. But it was too late. We heard barking. Not dogs. Their yaps were deeper than a mastiff's but sounded hollow. Unnatural and forced. They barked because that's what they were meant to do. It was inorganic. Like so much that was touched by vampirism, they sounded twisted. I'd faced their kind before, and they weren't a cake-walk.

I saw the black forms appear around a corner of the warehouse before us just before Henrik's head hit the ground. As they charged us, I saw their glowing red eyes, their unnaturally black fur and their hand-long fangs protruding out of their canine maws like some bad Halloween costume.

They were called lesser vampire hounds, but there was nothing lesser about them. Sure, they couldn't turn humans into vampires – that was what made them lesser rather than higher – but they could drain a human of all its blood all the same. I'd killed a lot of them in my line of work. I'd even saved Alex from a pack of them. Every single time, I'd almost died.

Brett and Guy jumped forward and opened fire. A hound fell. No yelp of pain. Not even a grunt. The only sign it was injured was that the red glow stopped. We'd still need to behead them. Vampires were all the same. Needed to stop that pesky regeneration. The rest of the hounds were bounding towards us. I heard the thuds of their paws like bowling balls hitting the concrete. They sounded louder than such a small creature had any right to sound.

They were closing in. The shots by Guy and Brett weren't having much effect and I could see that even Brett was shaking as he pumped out a used shell and fired again.

I was temporarily blinded by a flash of orange. Fire erupted in front of us and I heard the vampire dogs scream. I turned to see Pranish panting, swaying from side to side, his hand outstretched. He wasn't carrying a scroll. He'd memorised that spell. No wonder I saw puke and spittle seeping from underneath his mask. Recounting memorised spells was nauseating. You try memorising a nuclear bomb. No, not the concept. An actual literal nuclear bomb. That's what memorising a spell is like. The words are the power. Having those words in your head – it was like turning your brain into an arsenal. Not healthy.

The flames disappeared almost as quickly as they had appeared, as magical fire often did. Bullets flew at us as the fire dispersed. The sky decided to rain torrents at that moment as well. The four of us charged forward and came face to face with a horde of ghouls strapped with everything from cricket bats to Ak-47s.

We took cover behind a metal container, and then waited out the rain of lead and the cacophony of inhuman roars.

Henrik had been lying about there not being any guards, but I had not been sure by how much he'd been lying. I'd known this wasn't going to be easy, but I at least hoped I could do it. But with the grey hodgepodge horde before us, did we stand a chance?

Brett lay down fire but even he had to drop down behind the fortunate layers of metal containers we'd hidden behind in the warehouse lot. We hadn't even made it into the warehouse yet.

"How many are there?" Guy shouted over the chaotic orchestra of automatic rifles.

"About ten," Brett answered, pushing a round into his shotgun. He was struggling. Hands shaking. He'd still managed to get a count. It looked like an ocean to me.

Only ten?

I'd killed eight solo before. This time I had backup.

"Pranish, you got a shield?"

"One more," he panted, shuffling through his satchel. He took out a rolled-up scroll and held it to my forehead. He muttered a few words and it crinkled up into gold flames. I felt warmer. Like the sun had found a way to shine on me even in this stormy torrent.

"Make it count," he said.

I nodded, and made my way around the cover, opposite from the direction that the ghouls were shooting at. Brett and Guy opened fire blindly to distract them from my movements. I hoped that the metal containers would be enough to hold off the onslaught of lead.

"Act fast," Treth said, as if I needed reminding. "Even if they look human."

I stopped at the corner of the container, glanced at the flashes and amorphous grey humanoids, saw my opening and jumped to the next bit of cover.

What was Treth on about? I had killed plenty of things that look human. Killed plenty of ghouls. Killed a human, even. I didn't need his egging on.

I leapt to another metal container, behind the ghoul group. They were still opening fire intermittently. At least we had the right place. The Blood Cartel wouldn't give so much ammo to ghouls guarding any old warehouse. Trudie must be inside…if she was still alive.

From my vantage point, I could see the backs of the ghouls. They wore an assortment of clothes. The clothes they'd been ravaged in, probably. I gulped. This was what Treth was trying to warn me about. This hesitation. The ghouls had been human once. It was different from a vampire. A vampire had been human but had consented to the change. They were responsible for their actions. But ghouls – they had no choice. Who'd want to have all their blood drained, so they could be turned into mindless, monstrous thralls? Ghouls were victims. Just as much victims as zombies or any lesser undead.

They didn't ask for this, but I could help them in one way. I could end it.

I didn't have to sneak up on the ghouls. They were too busy reloading and firing on my friends. I ran, lifting my dual swords above my right shoulder, ready to deliver a clean beheading. I must not hesitate. Even if a ghoul is Trudie herself, I must not hesitate. Ever.

My feet beat on the wet concrete, and then my target turned. Its eyes glowed red and it snarled, even as its head fell to the ground. I ducked under the quick-fire reaction of a ghoul with an Ak-47 and brought my swords, now below my left armpit, up towards the assailant. My one blade clanked on the metal of the firearm, but the other found flesh. The attack sent the shots wide, piercing and staggering other ghouls who were attempting to close the gap towards me. None of them had close combat weapons. Only guns. Seems they didn't expect a swordswoman to close the gap. I felt a small vibration as Pranish's shield deflected a claw on my back. I stuck my sword behind me and pulled back. Felt resistance and the squelch as the blade found flesh. That'd keep the ghoul in pain for a bit. I kicked the ghoul in front of me, the one with the Ak and it dropped its rifle. I'd cut into its wrist and its hand was only holding on by some fleshy tendrils. I completed the artwork and sent its head to the floor. I felt more vibrations. More attacks. Thank Pranish and the local weyline! I needed more of these shield scrolls.

As I dived, ducked and struck the ghouls, my comrades moved forward, firing when there was no risk of hitting me. Shield or not, the kinetic force from a bullet would still hurt and could cause enough shock to still be fatal. The ghouls were no longer firing, instead forming a moshpit around me. Shots from Brett and Guy sent them staggering, allowing for quick beheadings.

And as was so often the case with fights, it ended. All the ghouls lay dead.

I cleaned my blades off on a ghoul's hoodie, panting my exertions away. Brett leaned down to pick up an Ak, passed it to Guy, passed another to Pranish and then picked one up for himself.

"I'd give you one," he said, "but you seem quite capable already."

I snorted in response. Brett continued.

"This looks like their forward guard. More vamps inside. They'll have better aim."

He looked at Pranish. "You ever fire a gun before?"

Pranish shook his head. He was holding the Ak like a pile of wood.

"Fire when I tell you. You aren't going to kill a vamp with that, but you can keep their heads down. Still hurts, despite the regeneration."

Pranish nodded. He'd played enough shooting games with Trudie and me to at least know the basics of firearms. Look down the sights and pull the trigger.

The warm glow dispersed as the shield ran out of juice. I felt the rain pelt my head, mask and shoulders. This fight had been easy, but the next wouldn't be. We were back into the firefight, and the vamps would be ready this time.

The warehouse was not the largest of the buildings, rising only slightly above one storey. Not enough for a second storey. Could all the people who had been abducted really fit in there? I remembered how slaves were transported across the Atlantic and I had to admit that it wouldn't be a hard task. That meant Trudie had been cramped like a sardine this entire time. Others would have been trapped for even longer.

The warehouse had a closed garage door, with a smaller service door next to it. A single light shone over the door. We couldn't go through it. The vamps would be waiting on the other site, guns trained on the doorway. It'd be a massacre.

"This warehouse is attached to a wharf," I said, peering through the rain. "That means there is an opening."

"You wanting a swim? With all your gear?" Brett said. It sounded like he wanted to chide me but wasn't in the mood for it himself. Neither was I.

"We go through that door and we're all dead. There may be a way to get onto the wharf and into the warehouse without having to swim and without attracting unwanted attention."

"Worth a shot," Guy chimed in.

We made our way to the edge of the warehouse, watching every angle for an attack. The hounds and ghouls hadn't been stealthy, but a vampire could be stealthy if they were so inclined. My scratchy bite-proof scarf would protect me for a few seconds, but the others were not so well prepared for a sneaky bite attack. In a split second, Pranish or the others could be dragged into the shadows and fed upon. In 24 hours, they'd rise up as a ghoul. That's if I didn't behead them first, and I would. They were my friends, and friends don't let friends become ghouls.

The warehouse lot gave way to a gentle slope strewn with rubble, ending with a turbulent sea below. Even in the dark, I could see the white foam assaulting the coast. Again, and again. For now, the coast survived, but given enough time – the sea would always win.

I looked up at the dark red sky. It was meant to be a full moon tonight, but the cloud cover was blocking the moon and stars. I hoped that'd disrupt the vampire's ritual in some way.

We scaled down the slope and made our way to the warehouse, but the warehouse stuck out, built on top of the water. We'd have to swim unless there was some sort of foothold. I approached the wall of the warehouse, splatter from the sea assaulting me like impotent shotgun pellets. There was a foothold. A small ledge separating the concrete foundation of the warehouse and its metal and brick-work walls. We'd be able to get in, slowly. But what if vampires were waiting on the other side?

Brett tapped my shoulder and I turned to huddle in with the others. In as quiet a whisper as he could articulate, Brett spoke.

"We need a distraction. Do you have any more detonation scrolls?"

Pranish shook his head. "But I do have a heat scroll. It'd melt a lock. But I thought we couldn't go through the front."

"We mustn't, but we need a distraction." He looked at Guy. "Take the wizard to the front. Make noise. A lot of it. We'll use the distraction to get in through the back."

We all nodded, and they left, leaving Brett and me. We got into position, our weapons stowed, and waited. First, we heard just a bang. Someone had slapped the garage door. Then, gunshots. I hoped that Pranish and Guy would be okay.

I lifted myself up first. It was a very small ledge and my toes stuck off the edge. I took a deep breath and sidled across the ledge towards the wharf entrance to the warehouse.

The cacophony from the front increased. I heart the ratta-tat-tat of Guy's machine pistols. At least he was still alive.

Brett followed me, and we sidled closer to the edge. I tried to listen to whatever was immediately inside but couldn't hear anything over all the other noise. I was going in blind and deaf. I hated that.

I finally rounded the corner, with tricky footwork, and landed on the wharf. Before me were around three vampires, all aiming their pistols at the single door to the wharf area. Two more vamps were carrying unconscious people into speedboats, piling them up like firewood. I didn't see Trudie among them. Was she already at the island?

Brett landed behind me and the vampires hadn't noticed yet. Brett tapped my shoulder and then indicated one of the pistol-wielding vamps close to us. He then indicated himself and another one further away. I nodded. He wanted me to get into position and take that one out. He'd fire when I had closed the gap.

I drew my swords as quietly as I could. One of the vamps twitched. I froze involuntarily. A cold drop of sweat formed on my brow. Nearer gunshots took the vamp's attention away. That was close. Guy and Pranish must've managed to get through, somehow.

I shifted closer, and closer to my target. Brett had taken some cover behind a crate and was aiming at his quarry. I hoped he was good enough of a shot. He needed to be quick. Two pistol guys out of range of my swords. He needed to drop both. Hopefully, the baggage carriers wouldn't be too big a threat. Vampires were always at least a little bit of a threat.

I was just behind my target when a vampire on the other side of the wharf cried out. I dived forward and skewered my target through the heart, beheading him with my other sword. Brett opened fire, switched, and opened fire again. Both his targets fell. One of the carriers pulled out a pistol and he opened fire on them. Missed. I dove for cover behind some metal barrels as two shots went wide and hit the headless vampire spitted on my one blade. Crouched, I retrieved my sword.

Brett's looted Ak clicked as he ran out of ammo and he seamlessly switched back to his shotgun. The carrier fell, but more vamps had arrived to back up the others. They all fell with bullets through the back of their heads. I didn't delay and went to behead them all. My blades were struggling. They needed to be sharpened. It had been a rough day for them.

Guy and Pranish appeared in the doorway. Pranish's satchel was much emptier and Guy was checking his last magazine.

"The front was not as guarded as we thought. Skeleton crew. But there's another wharf next door to this. We saw a vamp carry in one last person before coming here to back you up," Guy said.

I didn't delay any longer by speaking. I ran to the door they'd just gone through. They followed, and we jogged to the next door. It was ajar. I heard the rumble of a boat engine inside.

Trudie...

I kicked open the door and charged, almost mindlessly. The lone vampire inside was clutching a girl with raven black hair and smudged white and black makeup. Seeing me, he pulled the girl in front of him, to use as a shield.

But I didn't stop. I orientated my left shoulder towards Trudie and the vampire, and lifted my right behind my head, ready to thrust.

My heart beat. Slowly. Slowly. And the vampire was right in front of me. His red eyes were afraid. I saw his fangs, lusting after Trudie's exposed neck.

My blade found his face, and with it, I pulled him away from my friend, who fell onto the ground with a thud. The vampire clawed feebly at the air in front of it, squinting at the blade between his eyes. I took my free blade and placed it against his neck. Pulled back and swung. My blade was getting blunt. It didn't take his head off. Stopped at the spine. I chopped again. And again. And again. Until all the sinew was gone, and there was only a head spitted on my sword.

The others were right behind me. Pranish was bent over, examining Trudie.

"She's not waking up!" he cried.

Guy bent over her and felt her pulse. "She's alive. Vampire trance. She probably hasn't been awake since they caught her."

That was a relief. It was enough that Pranish and I were scarred. At least Trudie would not be able to remember this.

I felt my shoulders finally relax. Trudie was safe. And alive. Guy examined her more thoroughly and reported no bite wounds or other injuries. She was healthy and safe.

Brett was silent. I looked up at him. It wasn't like him to not relish a victory. His face was impassive, staring out towards the ocean. I looked where he was looking and tensed up again. The sky had cleared, and the full moon was above Robben Island. The island was glowing an unearthly blue, as chains from the moon fell down and sank themselves into the island.

We heard a hum, like a swarm of bees inside our heads, and then a crack and boom. A rift opened on Robben Island. A rift that we all knew couldn't mean well for any of us.

Chapter 21.   Island of the Ancients

"Go, Kat," Pranish said, cradling Trudie in his arms. His tears had stopped flowing ages ago, but his eyes were puffy and his face wet. His white hockey mask lay on the floor beside him. "I'll look after her."

"What if there are more vamps?" I asked. I couldn't take my eyes off the unearthly glow coming from Robben Island.

"I'll stay. You and Brett go," Guy replied. He had holstered his pistols and was carrying an Ak-47, stock nestled in his shoulder.

Brett was already taking his place at the wheel of the speedboat. I got in beside him. It was the first time I'd ever been on a boat and the rocking unnerved me. Not as much as the sight of those spectral chains and glow did, however.

Why was I doing this? Trudie was safe. I wasn't getting paid. The time to be a hero was over. My goal was achieved. Whatever this thing coming from the island was, it wasn't my business. I didn't have to risk my life any more.

But why then did I get in the boat, and why then did Brett start the engine and we sped off?

"I don't like that glow. It feels like evil," Treth said. "We have to stop it."

It was just that, wasn't it? It was the right thing to do. There was evil, and I needed to stop it.

I started this tale telling you how you shouldn't be a hero. You will be shunned. You will be hurt. You will die. And I'm a good authority on the matter. As every swell and bit of salt water hit us as we sped across the water to Robben Island and our very probable deaths, the very real thought of my own death was at the forefront of my mind. Yet, it meant very little. It would have to. You can't care simultaneously about your life and being a hero. You have to prioritise one of them.

So, take it from me. Don't be a hero. It's not a fate I would wish upon anyone I hold dear. Listen to me, as I know how bad it can be. I know I will die. I'll lie bruised, beaten and bleeding.

I will die.

And that will be that.

The shadowy shores of Robben Island, illuminated slightly by the alien glow of the anchors and vile energy, were fast approaching when we heard the screeches.

Horrific and bestial cries. I first thought of sirens, yet they were meant to sound entrancing. These shrieks made my blood go cold and my heart skip a beat. They were the screams of the honest predator. Dark airborne silhouettes approached us, flapping upon bat-wings. Yet they were not bats, or even vampire bats. They were the size of large men, with flowing dreads and teeth the size and shape of swords. Their skin was a mottled combination of red and ghostly white, with spots of ashen and coal grey. They carried no weapons but didn't need to. Their hands and feet were rakes and talons, as sharp and as brutal as their teeth.

"Take the wheel!" Brett shouted over the engine, the sea swells and the screeching.

I had never even driven a car before (except for my dad's car on the farm when I was really young. That didn't go so well), and boats were a different matter. I grabbed onto the almost car-like controls and held on, mustering all my strength to keep us centred on the shoreline. Brett took aim with his looted Ak and opened fire with the ammo he had retrieved at the wharf. A hail of bullets rang out towards the monsters looming down on us, but the effort was not even rewarded by a simple spray of blood, even though I could have sworn at least a few rounds found their mark.

"I thought I'd killed the last of you bastards!" Brett shouted, reloading and opening fire again. He must have seen these creatures before. They didn't look like any form of vampire I'd ever seen but, as Miriam would say, the more you learnt about vampires, the less you knew. They couldn't even be considered a species. I could only call them an affliction. A blight on life.

We were rushing ever closer to the shore and the creatures. Brett slung the Ak back around his back and pushed me away from the driver's seat. I gave him control and drew my swords just in time as a creature landed on top of us, its engorged and overly large teeth chomping on my blade. With my free sword, I stabbed at its chest, but my sword glanced off its steel-hard skin.

Brett took a hard turn with the boat, causing the creature to let go of my sword and fly back a few metres, ogling us with red, fish-like eyes. The turn ended abruptly as the boat met the resistance of a sandy shore and I almost lost my balance.

Three of the creatures hovered above us. They were silent, for a second, as I held my swords towards them and

Brett trained his shotgun and Ak at them, dual style. They screeched at us in unison and it took all my willpower to not cover my ears. It was a good thing I hadn't, as one of the creatures swooped down towards us and it was only my two swords that blocked the swipe of its rake-like feet. Brett opened fire on it, and while the blast of the shotgun didn't pierce its flesh, the impact did push it away.

"Keep going, Kat!" he shouted. It was one of the few times he'd said my name properly.

I deflected a blow from another of the creatures.

"What?!" I shouted back.

"Duck!" Treth yelled, and I did so. The creature landed in front of me, breaking through the side of the boat. I tried to stab it, but my sword clanged as if striking an anvil.

"I can handle these garkains. Keep going. Stop whatever they're doing!"

A wing from one of the creatures brushed up against me but it still felt like a punch. I hit the ground and saw Brett's boots appear before me in an instant. His shotgun blasted, and his Ak let out a strident melody. The blasts stopped for a second and he lifted me up.

"Go!" he said, looking me in the eyes. He was serious. Afraid, but very serious.

"You'll die!"

He forced a small grin. "I doubt it. I'm quite bad at dying."

He shoved me off the boat and onto the sand below. Two garkains looked at me, but quick blasts to their faces attracted their attention back to Brett.

"Go, Kat," Treth said. "Don't let his sacrifice be in vain."

My blades sank into the sand as I used them to help me up. I clambered forward, towards the light and away from the beach.

I wouldn't let Brett die. I'd stop all of this – whatever it was – and then come back to help him. I owed him that much.

I crossed over the threshold of sandy beach to rough foliage and was stopped by the blue light before me. It temporarily blinded me in its alien splendour and, when my eyes recovered, I couldn't believe what I saw. Colossal chains stretched as high as the moon itself and had pierced the ground like harpoons in a whale's flesh. Cracks in the

Earth formed spiderwebs from every chain and, between the monstrosities, a blue portal was opening from the ground not too far from me. Just over the next hillock.

What were they summoning?

"Nothing good," Treth said. More and more, I felt he could read my mind – or was getting very good at guessing what I was thinking.

"I don't know much about vampires," Treth continued. "But what I do know is as much as you – they are dangerous. Too dangerous to be allowed to live. Let's go. I'll watch your back."

I nodded, checked my swords for damage after their run-ins with the garkains. They had been blunted and chipped. I'd need to repair or replace them. But couldn't do that now. I advanced, damaged swords or not.

The sandy hill I had scaled from the beach descended onto a road pockmarked with potholes. I heard Brett's gunshots and the screeches of the garkains but not much else from any direction. Still, I advanced towards the centre of it all, crossing the street and stopping near a ruined face-brick hovel. There was no sign of life or un-life here. It was just another symbol of decay in this crumbling society. I went past the building and scaled the next hillock.

Before me was a well-lit area filled with as much activity as a stock exchange floor. People, wearing a variety of clothes, rushed between their respective stations. Many were at computers, typing away. Others were on cell phones. A circle of them looked to be meditating. Some held firearms, watching for invaders like me. The majority, however, were carrying bodies towards the centre of the activity, towards a crack in existence, from which I felt pure and unadulterated evil. An eldritch horror of cosmic darkness.

"You feel it?" Treth asked.

I gulped and nodded. I'm glad he had spoken. It distracted me from the feeling.

"I feel lives ending," he continued. "Every person who gets too close to that rift, is snuffed out. More than I was. Not even the spirit remains. They are deleted from existence. Fed upon until dry of even the essence of life."

I watched as another body was carried towards the rift, disappearing within it. One of those bodies could have been Trudie if we'd been too late. But even if Trudie was no longer among them now, they were still people. And they were dying. I couldn't waste any more time. Every moment was another life lost. So many lives lost already.

I no longer heard the gunshots from Brett. Only the screams. More winged vampires, looking more like demons than the vampires I knew, flew from the glow towards the beach and the city. I had a feeling that if I didn't do something soon, the casualties from the garkains and other vampiric beasts would be pitiful compared to what was to come. That pure evil within the rift felt intelligent. I detected its malice even across the divide of universes.

Could I kill something like that? Could I slay pure evil?

No, but I could stop it from coming through.

Pranish had taught me a bit about magic, and what he had taught me was that all magic had a cost. Sacrifice of energy, materials or life. And they also cost in the way of requirements. They needed the right tools, in the right formation, at the right time.

Flanking the rift were two columns of ancient stone, covered in a magical script unknown to me but reminiscent of claw marks. They glowed blue and red and throbbed with an un-biological heartbeat.

Demanzite, the powdered mineral that dispelled casting, didn't only work on human casters. It worked on enchanted items. While magic was being channelled, demanzite disabled it and harmed its user. If I could just throw the demanzite on those enchanted pylons, I could stop all of this. But how do I get there? The rift was in the centre of the activity. Tens, if not a hundred, vampires stood in my way. I had two swords and a dagger. And one sachet of demanzite in my front pocket.

How could I do it? It wasn't even a question of surviving. How could I get to the rift and be alive enough to disable it? I froze.

I could not. And every second that I could not, another person died, and that monster drifted ever closer into our world.

A deafening explosion shocked me out of my despair. Swathes of vampires collapsed as grenades were tossed from the darkness surrounding the lit area and into the horde.

The screeching from the garkains had stopped. And the gunshots were just beginning, on the other side of the expanse, where brief flashes showed me the bloodied form of Brett, firing his Ak into the vampires before him and stopping to throw a bandolier's worth of grenades.

I didn't stop to think. I bolted towards the rift, past dumbstruck vampires who were either rushing to the fight, or too distracted by it to notice me slip silently and swiftly past.

I kept sprinting, keeping myself low. Brett didn't stop. He relied on grenades to give him respite enough to reload. A gunshot ricocheted on a metal table near me and I dove away from it. A guard had spotted me and opened fire with a pistol. I threw my sword and the blade pierced his head. He dropped. It would take time to regenerate that. More vampires spotted me, and I sprinted full force to the rift, guards flying towards me and pale beasts charging me from every angle.

I tackled a vamp who hadn't stopped parcelling sacrifices into the rift. In a clean swipe, despite the damage to my blades, I cut off its head and continued running.

Closer. Closer. Closer.

The malice and anger only grew from the crack in space and time. This close, I felt an unchallenged fear. No zombie, no necromancer…nothing was so full of terror and unknowable horror as the alien evil seeping into our world through that crack.

I was terrified but had no time to cower. I had to shut it down. I had to end this. For Brett, who was flagging in his distraction. For Trudie, who had been saved just to have this thing seep into the world. For Hope City and the world.

I reached for the demanzite sachet in my front pocket, cracked open the paper seal and prepared to toss it at the rift and its pillars.

Metres away, I pulled back my arm and was stopped. I couldn't breathe as an arm of smoky and ethereal black lifted me up into the air. I noticed, out of the corner of my eye, that the vampires around me either stopped to stare at the aberration or began running away themselves. What could make such monsters so afraid?

The thought occurred to me instantly: their master.

I kicked my feet even as I dropped my sword and sachet of demanzite onto the floor pitifully. I kicked and I scratched at the hand around my throat, but to no avail. It was like clawing air. Evil, darkened air.

My vision blackened. Fear and suffocation was about to take me.

"Fight it!" Treth shouted, and my eyes opened. A pair of fangs, the size of a humanoid vampire's, floated before me. They were approaching my neck, savouring the moment. Slowly, ever closer. Like a tentative lover. They meant to feed. To suck me dry, or to turn me into an abomination – I didn't know.

But I wouldn't let them.

I will not be a monster's meal!

"I will not be a monster!"

I didn't know if it was me or Treth who had shouted both. Only that the yell, somehow breaking through the spectral arm around my throat, had made the fangs hesitate. They recovered and approached again. They came ever closer, savouring the moment. It enjoyed a helpless meal, but also relished the challenge of a feisty victim. The fangs stroked against my neck, as cold as ice. I felt a stab through my heart and my breath caught in my throat.

I felt coal in my veins. The same feeling that I'd had when the necromancer from North Road, the one who helped me learn about Trudie's whereabouts, cast dark magic on me. I hadn't really had coal in my veins. All I had felt was a cold and intense darkness within me. A pain beyond what was natural. A pure evil.

I felt it now, as these mist-like teeth considered my neck a mere lamb to be slaughtered.

But I am no lamb.

I fight the darkness. I stare evil down. I survive every atrocity put against me. I have lived through too much to die now. I've made too many promises. To others, to Treth, to myself. I've got too many quests. Too many plans. And I know I can handle them. Cause I've done it all before, and I've looked death in the eyes a thousand times, and I've never blinked. And this was no different. This was just a monster, and I slay monsters.

My heart stopped, and my mouth opened unconsciously. The words that came out were not English or any language I recognised. But yet, I understood every word. They were filled with a power that made me understand the primordial spells of wizardry. They told a story of power in every syllable and they carried forth a will to move mountains.

And Treth and I shouted together, our words of power, of will and purification. Words that neither of us had ever heard before but didn't need to. The words flooded out, yet I didn't think of any of them. They came as primal words of nature. They had existed within me before all this. They were as natural as breathing. They were the ancient words of purity that existed within all good things.

The fangs retreated and attempted to charge between every incantation. I stared at them and saw through their misty façade. I saw power. Deep and bottomless power. The evil that rests within existence manifest. But evil, no matter how undiluted, can be defeated.

Together, Treth and I shouted, in English but with a will even stronger than the primordial words before. We shouted:

"We fight the darkness. We are the light."

The fangs tried to make another break towards my neck. I exposed it, taunting it. The fangs stopped and hissed against the invisible wall of power that surrounded us.

"Foul thing," we shouted in perfect unison. I had never heard Treth's voice so clearly. I could swear he was speaking truly aloud and not just within my head. "You have no place within our realm. Go back to the darkness. Go back and disperse within your own chaos."

The fangs stopped. Floated.

I stared at it, in the silence. The intelligence behind the incorporeal being considered me. It looked for weakness. It found none.

"We hold the line, monster," I said. "Leave."

The fangs froze and dispersed. It sank back into the rift. The spectral arm loosened, and I dropped onto the ground, scraping my knees.

The anger from the eldritch abomination on the other side of the rift grew. It approached, to fight me directly. It shot out a wave of pure fear. It meant to terrify me into paralysis. I was not afraid. I stood up and placed my hands on either pillar.

"Stay in your hole, monster," I said, and with a temporary bout of inhuman strength, I pushed.

The pillars resounded with an unnatural boom as they hit the sandy floor below. The rift burst out into an explosion that didn't harm me but sent every vampire in the vicinity reeling. Those who didn't shut their eyes and hit the deck, glowed red on their necks, where they had been turned. They screamed as I smelt the burning flesh. They clawed at their necks, drawing blood and ripping off skin. Those with claws capable of doing so, ripped out their own throats. So, agonising was their pain, that through sheer desperation, their regeneration was shut down. They fell to their wounds, and they didn't get back up. In a way, it was mercy.

All the vampires just outside of range stared at their tortured kin and fled. There was no point fighting anymore. Their master was banished back to its realm, and their kindred had fallen to its last fit of anger. Unable to strike at me, the horror tortured its minions. Such was the way of evil. Hopefully, the surviving vampires knew this. They had lost this battle that hadn't been worth fighting. We had won. For all that was worth.

Chapter 22. Regrets

Trudie didn't remember a thing about the abduction. Last thing she remembered was arguing with Stephanie over punk-rock at the lounge and then waking up in a hospital bed. This time, it was me standing alongside Pranish at her side.

She had no wounds. No scars to remember her ordeal. She didn't recall a damn thing, and, for that, I was relieved. The loss of her recent friend, Stephanie, was only a small sadness. The type of loss you can get over, eventually.

"How could you do all that?" she scolded, looking very normal yet abnormal without her goth make-up.

Pranish and I just grinned. It was good old Trudie. Our friend. She'd nag and nag but, because she loved us, and we loved her back. To see her smile made it all worth it. But, we didn't smile at each other when she wasn't looking. We both saw it in each other's eyes. Pranish had always seen it in my eyes, but it was the first time he understood what it was, and the first time I'd seen it in his. It was a blankness. A greyness that came from seeing too much in too little time. Trudie may not remember any of this, but Pranish would. Forever.

We all left the warehouse and the island before anonymously tipping off multiple major television stations. The Council may have ignored the tip-off, but the ever-hungry media could be relied upon to generate a stinker. Rescue crews were soon brought to ferry the survivors to clinics in Hope City. Vampire experts and agencies stayed to examine the sites but, without having been there, they had no real knowledge of what had happened.

Drake, the private investigator, and many of the mimic's other victims, were found alive in the warehouse and in the piles of bodies being prepared for sacrifice. He had thanked me for continuing his investigation, and for saving him. I had thanked him. Without his notes, I'd have never stopped the mimic. Wouldn't have believed that it was a mimic. I would have walked into that warehouse expecting some sort of other monster and then been eaten by a crate. Natalie cornered me on the way to visit Trudie and had given me a sincere apology for not having faith in me, and huge thanks for saving her husband. I refused her extra payment. I had been paid for that job already. I felt Treth have some extra pride in me then. It wasn't like I was doing it for him though. I was a professional. I got paid for a job. Didn't need gifts.

As I had promised, I reported everything to LeBlanc. She used the information to finish her book – revolutionising vampire lore. It was still a fringe theory, but LeBlanc had her fan clubs in academia. Within the next few years, the Ancients theory would become common curriculum. LeBlanc believed that the rift had been a portal to a plane she referred to as the *Dark World*, the home world of the vampire. The vampires on Earth, for whatever reason, were trying to attract an original vampire to Earth with human essence and sacrifice. It couldn't just be the simple gangsterism that led the vampires of the Blood Cartel to do such a thing. It was something much more sinister and, while LeBlanc hadn't written this in her book, she told me, in confidence, that she believed that the vampire affliction did more than just mutate its host. It was a contract. A hierarchy. And at the top of the hierarchy was a dark god, looking for openings into living worlds from which to feed.

This was all unconfirmed, however, but LeBlanc assured me that I had, in all likelihood, stopped an ancient vampire from entering Earth. I'd saved Hope City, if not the world.

But, at what cost?

While I had been chasing vampires, swathes of the slums had been annexed by a new Necrolord. Gangs that didn't swear undying fealty were wiped out and risen as the truly undying. Countless innocents disappeared. A shadow had descended on the slums of Hope City. The vampires may be licking their wounds, but the undead had risen to new heights.

I couldn't help but feel that while one fought one evil, another would always triumph. This was a game of whack-a-mole, and I didn't have enough mallets.

Andy phoned me the next day to apologise for not helping. He didn't answer any of my questions, however. Didn't even make an excuse. He just said sorry and asked me to send my regards to Trudie. I didn't forgive him. Never did. His presence among the friend group became rarer and rarer. When Trudie asked why I gave him such cold looks, I answered.

"Because he didn't help."

She only frowned and lit another cigarette.

The vampire barman from the Quantum had survived the attack, somehow. Regeneration was something even LeBlanc was not certain about. It was hard to do lab tests on vampires, so we didn't know the extent of their abilities.

All I knew was that the vampire appeared on the news the following days and spoke about hate crimes against his race. CCTV footage of the four of us raiding the Quantum appeared all over the news. We scrapped our gear with the help of Conrad and had to buy new masks. We were only lucky Guy and Brett had been in unmarked armour. Drakenbane hadn't taken them to task for anything. No Council tick had come knocking on Pranish or my door's either. While plenty of people knew we had knocked over the Blood Cartel at the warehouse and on Robben Island, they were the types of people who kept things like this hush-hush. They knew that it wasn't prudent to be a hero.

Luckily, it took only a week for naïve public sympathy to die down for the owner of the Quantum. It didn't help his cause that there were thirty survivors from Robben Island to attest to the malice of vampires. Thirty survivors were not enough, I couldn't help but think. Especially with the death tolls coming in from the slums. Thirty was just a drop in the water compared to all the people who had died, and all the people who still died in the slums.

I did what I could, as I always had, to stem the undead, but even I grew weary of the zombies. The number was so great that the city stopped paying bounties for them. They couldn't risk going bankrupt. Had to keep lining their own pockets and keeping the Titan asleep.

So, with a heavy heart, I arrived from a cheap job at the frontier between slum and suburb and lay my new gear on the floor of my apartment. Duer woke for a second to greet me and then went back to bed. Alex was asleep too. Trudie had come in earlier to feed and play with him.

I was peeling my sweat-stained clothing off my clammy skin when the phone rang, and my heart stopped. I didn't think I could be afraid to hear the tune of *Charming Man* by The Smiths. I checked the number and it was unknown. My breath caught in my throat, but I still clicked the receiver and brought it to my ear.

"Congratulations, Kat," a deep voice, rumbling with modulated static, spoke. It chilled me to the bone as it had before.

I didn't reply.

"Come now, Kat. It isn't every day that you save the world. Celebrate!"

"Why?" I asked, simply.

"Why what? Why did I help you?"

A pause, and then a laugh. Filled with what I imagined to be equal measures of malice and mirth. "A trade, Kat. For the info you needed to save your friend, the city and the world, you only needed to leave me in peace. It was a fair trade, if you ask me. I'm sure that your good friend, Trudie, appreciates it, even if she acts as if you should have let her die."

How did the voice know so much?

"You went the extra mile, Kat," it continued. It sounded happy. Proud of itself. "And while the trade has already been concluded, I feel I can grant you a gift."

"I don't want anything from you."

"You should be more careful…" The voice ignored me. "Where you look for favours. Not everyone is as trustworthy as me. The Council, for instance. Don't you find it odd that it ignored this entire matter?"

I held my tongue. They had my attention now.

"There are much more than just spooky ghosts and violent beasts in Hope City, Kat. There's something much deeper roiling below the surface of this teetering city.

Something much darker than a humble necromancer like myself. Choose your friends wisely going forward. Trust your instincts. And stay alive. I'd like to play a little bit more in the future. This friendship has only just begun."

The necromancer laughed, and I hung up.

"We'll catch them," Treth said.

I wasn't so sure.

I looked out the window of my apartment. I could see the lights of Hope City, beacons in a sea of nightly darkness.

I loved and hated this city, and I wasn't going to let some necromancer, or anyone else, take it from me.

Afterword

I tend to only write the afterword for a book long after I've finished its first draft. It gives me time to think. Time to stew. And it lets me read the story as if I am just a reader, and not its author.

Kat goes through some fundamental changes through this book. I believe that the story does become darker, continuing the trend at the end of book 1. I also believe, however, that this darkness doesn't sacrifice what makes this series and Kat's adventures essentially enjoyable. She's still the snarky badass with a heart of gold. And that's what I love about her.

And I hope you do too.

Acknowledgements

While books are (often) the work of a single person, they take a veritable organisation to produce. I'm an independent author because I value my freedom and am sceptical of the traditional publishing industry. While this makes some aspects of my business easier, it also means that I lack a certain connection to an institution. Succinctly: this is a lonely career.

But there are people in my life who have helped me along and have been integral to the creation of this book and series.

It takes a lot of patience to write six books before releasing a single one, and without the feedback and conversation of my beta readers, Tyler Sudweeks and Chelsea Murphy, I would have gone insane a long time ago. Thank you!

I would also like to thank my mother for providing her editing skills to get these books into a condition fit for human consumption, and for being someone I can always natter to about Kat, Hope City and necromancy.

Thank you to Deranged Doctor Design for the wonderful cover art. I advise them to any author looking for a professional design.

And finally: thank you. Without you, this book would not be read and enjoyed. Without you, these words are just the scribblings of a half-mad author.

So, thank you!

And until next time.

Nicholas Woode-Smith is a full-time fantasy and science fiction author from Cape Town, South Africa. He has a degree in philosophy and economic history from the University of Cape Town. In his off-time, he plays PC strategy games, Magic: The Gathering, and Dungeons & Dragons.